DOCTOR WHO

REVOLUTION MAN

PAUL LEONARD

Published by BBC Worldwide Ltd,
Woodlands, 80 Wood Lane
London W12 0TT

First published 1999
Copyright © Paul Leonard 1999
The moral right of the author has been asserted

Original series broadcast on the BBC
Format © BBC 1963
Doctor Who and TARDIS are trademarks of the BBC

ISBN 0 563 55570 X
Imaging by Black Sheep, copyright © BBC 1999

Printed and bound in Great Britain by Mackays of Chatham
Cover printed by Belmont Press Ltd, Northampton

For my mother

Hazel Hinder-Bunting

*with thanks for all your love
and support over the years,
without which none of my
books could have been
written.*

Prologue

'I don't agree,' said Sam.

The Doctor looked at her with that puzzled expression – eyebrows raised slightly, hands spread wide – which Sam knew meant he was open to suggestions. His jacket was unbuttoned, and he wasn't wearing his waistcoat; his hair looked even wilder than usual. Sam decided he was worried. Even so…

She glanced over at the library doorway, but there was no sign of Fitz. He seemed to be fascinated by the books, and could spend hours in there – but Sam had known there was something wrong when the Doctor had suggested that Fitz go in search of a book.

'We should tell Fitz what we're doing,' she said. 'We know there might be trouble –'

'But we don't know what sort!' The Doctor gestured at the display above the console. It showed a representation of the vortex. Sam knew the patterns well by now, the translation schematics, and she could see something was wrong. More worrying still was the place – Earth – and the date – June 1967, Humanian Era. The Doctor jumped up to point at individual distortions on the screen. 'All I know is that these discontinuities seem be linked to a certain type of event.'

He ran around the console, his feet skidding on the floor. Sam followed a little more carefully, testing the grip on her new boots. She'd bought them in a corner store on the fringes of a desert, under a bloated red sun and a sky spangled with space stations. She'd had no idea where or when she was, but the boots were heavy, chunky, practical, and had fitted magnificently. She'd paid with amber beads, and the trader had seemed happy enough.

The Doctor was looking at a screen that showed an extraordinary picture: one of the Egyptian pyramids, with a huge, new carving made in one stone face – a crude capital R in a circle. It was a TV report, in black and white with a low-resolution scan. An earnest young man in a suit was babbling into a large microphone about 'the activities of the so-called Revolution Man'.

She frowned. 'That never happened!' she said after a while. 'I'm sure I would have –'

The Doctor glanced at her. 'I know. It's an anomaly. The earliest ones are quite small, but this is very big – big enough to be a threat to Earth's timeline.'

'I thought it had more than one.'

'It does, sort of. I've contributed quite a few complications around this period in Earth's history. I don't think the vortex will take much more.' He gave her one of his brilliant smiles, as if this were an academic matter, a point that needed illustrating, rather than a threat to the existence of her home planet.

'Perhaps you're the Revolution Man,' Sam suggested, only half joking. 'In a later incarnation. Or even an earlier one, and you've forgotten about it. Perhaps you're fighting the Sontarans out there, and this is an unforeseen side effect.'

But the Doctor just shook his head. 'I wish I was. Then at least I'd have a chance of knowing what was going on. This looks purely mischievous – but it could be serious, Sam.'

'Which is all the more reason why Fitz should know what we're doing,' offered Sam patiently.

'Take it from me: it's better that he doesn't. If he knew, it could make things worse. There are too many things he doesn't understand yet. It's too complicated.'

Sam glanced at the library door again, then at the screen. 'I don't agree,' she repeated, but she knew she probably wouldn't tell Fitz. Not if the Doctor was so sure it wasn't a good idea.

Not yet, anyway. Not unless things got desperate.

But then, they usually did.

Book One
1967

Chapter One

White. For the rest of her life Maddie would associate that moment with white. Not the dirty, slightly marbled white of the stone sink, or the enamelled white of the cooker, or the painted white of the fridge (on which stood a small black-and-gold PYE radio, its tinny speaker issuing the words she had half expected but didn't want to believe), but a hard and perfect white, searching, impossible, a white that hurt her eyes and hurt her brain.

The white of Himalayan snow in the sun. The sun-etched white of Ed's face towering above the mountains, his body arched across the sky, his feet far away on the world's blue rim, and the terror, the terror in his voice: *you shouldn't have done that, baby, oh my God you shouldn't have done that –*

And there was blood on the ball of her finger, just a tiny spot, like an insect, less than an insect, and then it was gone.

Darkness. In that morning, in that terrible white light in the kitchen, she would remember the darkness. The innocence of it, the comfort. The darkness behind the blindfold, her bare feet on a wooden floor, the smell of varnish and paint. The safe feel of Ed's hands on her shoulders, steering her as if she were his little motor scooter, his Vespa. He even squeezed her shoulder when he wanted her to stop, making her shoulder blade into a brake lever. Obedient, she halted, but then was overcome with curiosity and reached out with one foot, moving it slowly, carefully, in case there was anything hard. Maddie felt the soft, silky surface of... an eiderdown? A cushion?

'OK.' Ed's voice was close to her ear. She could feel his breath, smell the garlic, black pepper and ginger. What had he called that stew? Tie-Koo? His hands were at the back of her head, untying the blindfold. 'You can look now.'

The blindfold dropped, revealing candlelight. A bed, in front of her, the counterpane quilted with primary colours, candles on a sill above it, a dark window, sloping inward. Misted reflections of the candle flames hung like a chain of fuzzy golden planets. Maddie blinked, turned her head, drew a breath.

The loft was huge. The beams were painted, each one different: orange, yellow, red, purple, green. A brick pillar in the centre – the chimney stack? – was sprayed with more colours, stick men, graffiti, crude flowers.

'Look at this – I did this for you!' Ed's hand was turning her head, his fingers on her cheek strangely cold. She saw a stained-glass window built into the roof, a red and crystal bird, dimly lit from the inside, so that the red was like blood. It flew over emerald fields, through a sapphire sky, towards a topaz sun. Highlights from the candle flames were scattered across the scene like sundust.

'Wow!' Maddie stared and stared. 'Where did you get –' But Ed's cold fingers were on her cheek again, steering her vision.

'Look!'

She saw hanging candles, a wooden Buddha, waist-high, cross-legged and creased with black fat, his face long and somnolent. There was a fresh flower in his lap. Was it a shrine? Ed had told her he'd become a Buddhist, but she'd thought he was joking. The flower was a carnation, pink and

8

red, the ragged patterns and folds of its petals as intricate as a fingerprint. She could almost feel it from here, touch its flowery scent. She stepped forward to pick it up, thought better of it, then made a little bow to the Buddha.

Ed laughed. 'He's Lamaist, not Theravada.'

Maddie felt herself blush, but she wasn't about to ask for an explanation. She didn't want to seem stupid in front of this leather-clad Jesus, her man. His band had a record in the Top Thirty. If she seemed stupid, he might lose interest. Then she would just be an art-school girl again, a pastel painter without a bit of talent, not quite rich enough to be independent, and too long-legged to be attractive.

The bongo drums had started again downstairs. She could hear her sister, Emma, her voice fast and earnest. Probably talking to Ron, the band's drummer, about Vietnam, or Cuba, or somewhere like that. They both seemed to be interested in that sort of thing. A faint clash of strings, then the twanging of the sitar – was Ron playing it? There was a candle in front of the Buddha, the flame flickering, almost burned out.

'You haven't seen it all yet.' Ed's hands were on her shoulders again, pushing her forward, around the pillar, past the Buddha. Her feet almost tangled on the floor, and his grip tightened, to steady her, pulling her against him. She wondered if he was going to make love to her now. No. Ball. That was the word he used. Have fun. Have a ball. Don't get too heavy about it. Keep it laid back.

She wanted to do that. But instead he let her go, stood there, letting her see –

Black. Black beams, black floor, a black iron hat stand. On top of the hat stand, above eye level, there was a skull. Not human: long-jawed, small-eyed, a candle burning between the eyes. A goat? It was surrounded by lumps of charred bone hanging in midair, apparently unsupported.

'Life and death,' said Ed.

'Mmm.' Maddie was *determined* not to be shocked. But the skull was creepy. She'd rather look at the Buddha. She looked over her shoulder at the carved wood. The Buddha's face seemed to be frowning at her, or maybe that was a wink in the dancing candle flame.

Ed took her hand. 'Don't be afraid. The Great Wheel goes on turning. Shambala, Shiva, Om-Tsor: they're all the same. That's what they told us out there in Nepal. That's where this room is. A space that shows you life and death.'

'Mmm,' said Maddie again. Reluctantly, she turned back to look at the skull. It was small, the surface papery. The wall behind it was black, even the joists painted over. A space without stars, without light, without possibilities.

Ed let go of her hand. There was a faint creaking of springs as he sat down on the bed. 'Hey, you know what happens between life and death,' he said.

Maddie turned to face him. Big, a big animal, looking up at her, his face confident and powerful. But the skull worried her. She didn't like the skull. She remembered walking with Emma last summer, out beyond the road into the long grass. They'd been going to have a picnic. Then there'd been this *thing*, this lump of white wool and crawling black things. Dead. A dead sheep. It was the flies that she remembered. The hordes of flies, their blackness, the sudden roar as they lifted from the corpse.

Ed's hands were on her hips. 'What's the matter, baby? Scared?'

Maddie stepped back. 'No.' It was more complicated than fear, she thought. Too complicated to explain. 'I just - don't want to do it now.' She heard Emma laugh, a whinnying sound, and grabbed the excuse. 'Not with the others downstairs.'

Maddie was amazed at how prissy her voice sounded, and wasn't surprised when Ed laughed. 'You're not at West Kensington High School for Young Ladies any more, Mads,' he said. 'Emms isn't your form monitor.' He plucked at the collar of his leather jacket. 'And I'm not wearing my Eton tie.'

Maddie stepped back. 'All the same, I'd rather get back downstairs. But thanks for showing me this room.' Turning, she saw the coloured bird again and realised that the material wasn't stained glass at all, but cellophane stuck to ordinary glass. She could see the tape holding it in place. Perhaps the goat's skull was made of paper. Perhaps the bones were fakes, too. Perhaps everything was a fake.

Perhaps. She heard Ed get up off the bed, felt him grab her around the stomach.

'Come on, baby, you're my girl, aren't you?' His voice was in her ear, his body pressed against her back, and she could smell the garlic and ginger on his breath again. It seemed to have gained a sour edge.

'I'd rather go back down.' Again, Maddie was shocked at how prissy her voice sounded, how like the schoolgirl she was determined to outgrow. Downstairs, Emma laughed again. The bongo drums stopped, though the sitar continued - dull, crudely plucked notes.

Ed's grip tightened. His arms were like ropes, binding her stomach. 'Hey, it was OK last time, wasn't it?'

'It was fine,' said Maddie, quickly. 'I just -'

He let her go. 'You need to relax a bit, baby. Hang loose.' He got up off the bed, walked past her to the chimney breast. 'Let's walk in the mountains.'

It was the title of the band's Top Thirty song, and he was half singing it, repeating the mantra. It was like being there at the moment of creation, even though the song was already recorded. The drums started up again, like the pulse of the universe. When Ed removed a brick from the chimney breast, Maddie half expected the roof to open above her, the beams to unfold like the petals of a flower, and the sky above to be full of colours.

Colours. In the morning, after the words on the small black-and-gold PYE radio, in that Himalayan whiteness of the kitchen, she remembered the colours she had hoped for with a bitter clarity. The world had seemed a child's toy twelve hours before, a rainbow beach-ball planisphere full of beautiful light and beautiful music and her beautiful man: now it was revealed as hell, white hell, the clear day on which you can see for ever.

What had her mother said? 'Just one mistake…' But she'd been talking about sex, of course. It seemed laughable, now. All that worry, all that guilt, those screaming rows: 'He's a long-haired lout and I don't care how good you think his music is; he's a singer, just a singer, and don't you know you deserve better than that?'

Oh, it seemed so silly. What she deserved. What she didn't deserve. There was only one thing that she deserved now, and that was –

– blood on the ball of her finger, a tiny spot, like an insect –

12

She turned, then, turned from the white kitchen and the white light and the radio now chattering about the test match, and made the dark walk through the passage and up the stairs, up the ladder into the loft which was dark and rich with colours and the petals still in the cups, the *petals*, white as ice.

She forced herself to look away, to see Ed lying across the bed, half covered by the counterpane. She sat down on the bed, shook his shoulder, and told his bleary morning eyes, told the red dark shadows in his brain, that, yes, it had happened, that they weren't dreaming, that it was on the radio so it must be the truth.

They looked at each other for a long time, then he staggered upright, his eyes confused and perhaps empty. Jesus naked, Jesus betrayed. Maddie stared down at the white petals, trying to blame them.

I didn't believe it was real…

Petals. Ice-white petals.

'Wings plucked from celestial butterflies,' Ed informs her, swaying slightly as he holds the wooden box in front of her. It's a quote from the song. They still look like petals to Maddie, pressed petals of incredibly white roses. 'They carry the life essence, the spirit of nirvana.'

Maddie looks at the whiteness, her eyes drown in it. She is given the box to hold. It feels rough, ancient. She can feel history in its contours, in the black-bruised carvings nubbly under her fingers, carrying soft stories full of stars and magic.

Ed goes down the ladder. 'We need a kettle.'

She holds the box of petals or celestial butterflies. They

seem to glow. She hears talking downstairs, Ron's voice, '*No,*
Ed. You're *not.*'

And Ed: 'She's my girl, OK? I trust her, OK?'

Maddie feels a glow, a glow from her face to her toes. He
trusts me, he *trusts* me, he really, really *does*. This is real
magic I'm holding in my hands; this is the real magic he
brought back from the East and he trusts me with it.

Ed's face rises from the trapdoor, smiling. He's holding a
kettle in one hand, an ancient tin kettle with a curl of steam
emerging into the cool air of the attic, and two white cups
in the other. They clink together, one, two, three times.
Maddie smiles at Ed.

He puts the teacups in front of the Buddha, puts the petals
in the teacups, pours on the water. The fluid fizzes, glows,
like celestial lemonade. Maddie is enchanted.

'This is Om-Tsor, Maddie. Say it.'

'Om-Tisor,' says Maddie.

'Om-*Tsor*. T-zz-awr. The magic mantra.' He's singing the
song again.

Then he hands her the cup.

'Drink it.'

And she does.

Later, much later, she tried to tell herself that she should have
known. That she should have guessed as soon as she felt the
teacup, cold in her hands. As soon as the fizzing liquid
touched her lips, ice-cold even though the water from the
kettle must have been near boiling. But all she could
remember thinking was, *This is the real magic dust, this is
the real thing*. The drink was like a lake in the mountains,
spouting geysers that glittered in the candlelight. Liquid

tickled her nose.

When she drank, her throat went numb. For a moment, her mind was full of colours, numbers, lights…

Then she was flying. Flying above the mountains.

The air was incredibly cold, the buckled land below her sharp and granular – it was as if she could see each individual crystal that made up the wind-etched snow fields, each particle of grit and stone flowing inside the gnarled ice of the glaciers. When she breathed, the air was like knives. She wasn't afraid of falling, because she wasn't falling.

She saw Ed, smiling at her as he materialised against the royal-blue sky. His hair rippled in the wind, as if it were a forest growing on a hill. Sunlight blazed on his face, leaving black shadows.

'"In the mountains, there you feel free",' he said, then pointed behind her. 'Look!'

She turned, felt air buffet her, saw the sun blazing white over a purple distance. Squinting into the light, she saw a deep valley, a darkness, a mist, a hint of green forest. She began swimming at the air, clumsy, trying to move herself towards the warmer world.

Then she thought, *This is an illusion. I don't need to make any effort. Just* be *there*.

And she was there, suspended in mist that for a moment felt warm, then turned clammy. She could see the heads of trees poking up through the mist, perfect, moss-headed, speckled with the warm, heart-beating dots of birds. She could hear the chatter of water on stone, the hiss and rumble of a waterfall.

Down, Maddie thought; *Let's see the river*.

And she was standing beside it, as tall as the trees. The mist had gone: no, that wasn't true. It was still there, she could track each watery particle of it, but she could see through it as well, the grey water quivering over rocks and grit and sand, the fish, cold-eyed, quick, moving, the rope bridge –

Rope bridge!

She took a step towards it, saw the river water explode into spray as her huge foot touched it. *Poor fish*, she thought, even though they were illusions. She made herself bigger again, floated above the bridge, saw movement on the grey sheer slope of the mountain – a train!

A tiny, perfect steam train, with a plume of dirty smoke and wheels spinning, and pistons like miniature sewing needles, glinting in the sun. The carriages tatty, tawdry, orange-and-green and – yes – those were people! Hanging from the carriage windows, even clinging to the white wood-slatted roofs, hundreds and hundreds of people, and she could feel their faces, their hearts, their flesh, smell their sweat and the grey steam smuts of the engine –

'Mads! Hey, baby!'

She looked round.

Ed, against the sky, a giant with a shadowed face.

'Mads, we shouldn't be here. You have to stay in the mountains. That's what they told me. You have to stay in the mountains or you can't get back.'

Worried, Maddie moved –

– *touched* –

– touched the rock, like a rock on a beach, rough grained stone and a faint coldness, just for an instant, a slight ledge, and she turns back and sees the crumbled stone, her finger where the sharp rail has broken and the train –

- the train is falling, carriages crumpling -

- she grabs at the carriages, feels them crush under her fingers, feels the pain: bones breaking, flesh pulping, hearts stopping. The engine explodes, a slow flower of amber and soot and ashes, torn metal flying and cutting -

- cutting people, people dying, bursts and flashes of agony -

The carriages fall into the valley, crushing the trees and the birds and the people. The last carriage falls from Maddie's fingers and skids on the rock, bouncing once, twice, and then coming to rest in the settling dust, a broken, buckled toy. They are dead, all dead, and she knows they are dead and the last ones are dying and this is real it must be real and please, please, please let it be an illusion -

And Ed is saying it, 'You shouldn't have done that, baby. Oh my God, you shouldn't have done that.'

And there is blood on the ball of her finger, just a tiny spot, like an insect, less than an insect, and then it is gone.

'Reports are reaching us of a major train disaster in northwestern India. Details are still sketchy, but it appears that several hundred people may have died after a derailment in the Vale of Kashmir, in the Himalayas.

'And now for the latest news of the test match, over to our sports correspondent -'

Chapter Two

This was the year when London became another city, a space echoing with Eastern harmonies and decorated in primary colours, screaming with Beatlemania, thudding with the deep, sensuous beat of the Rolling Stones. For a year and a day, the bombed-out capital of a fallen empire became nirvana, the dream destination, the place to which the young people followed the Pied Piper of fashion and the rich scent of incense and lived in a multicoloured dream of old stone and jasmine gardens, hash smoke and red buses, bowler hats and revolution.

Or so the Doctor had said – but he must have been in one of his more poetic moods. The place smelled just the same to Fitz. An old, tired city: wet stone, petrol, diesel, tobacco, beer, coal smoke and sewage.

It was night. They were walking somewhere near Earl's Court station, the TARDIS parked outside, masquerading, as it had when he had first seen it, as a real police telephone box. Sam and the Doctor were ahead, pointing at the bright windows of the restaurants, the garish Formica tables, oohing and aahing as if they'd never seen the capital of the United Kingdom before. Inevitably, it was raining: a steady drizzle, fine enough to find its way through the collar of Fitz's trench coat, yet heavy enough to make slick puddles on the dented pavement. Fitz made awkward steps over them. Ahead, the Doctor ignored the water, and Sam kicked at it, sending brief sprays into the air. She was wearing green waders with yellow tops, like a toddler in a park.

His voice drifted back: '…Yetis in the underground?'

Sam spoke, her first words lost in the growl and hiss of a passing taxi. '…regeneration?'

'Yes, yes. The Brigadier was most confused, poor chap.'

Fitz felt the usual pang of annoyance. Sam and the Doctor always had so much to talk about. When Sam talked with Fitz it was a game, a dance, it was about winning and losing and being clever. Sam and the Doctor seemed able to talk without that happening. Perhaps that was because they'd known each other so long: but Fitz suspected it was something else, something to do with his own personality. Or lack of one. Steadily over the last few weeks, Fitz had begun to feel a little excluded, as if he'd been an interesting novelty which was beginning to lose its appeal. If that was the word. If that had ever been the word. He sighed. He was probably just feeling out of his depth again. Time to wade in regardless – it seemed to work for the Doctor, after all.

He trotted forward, grabbed the Doctor's arm and said in his best Alfred Dolittle accent, 'Local guide, sir! Local guide, honest chap, guv'nor! Only sixpence ha'penny an hour!'

Sam laughed, but the Doctor turned round, doffed an invisible hat, and said, 'Kind sir! You're the very person we need! Can you tell me the shortest way to Piccadilly Circus?'

Fitz thought for a moment, then said, 'Oughter use the tube, matey. Piccadilly line.'

'Just what I said,' put in Sam. 'But the Doctor's afraid of Yetis.'

Fitz didn't hesitate. 'The 'bominable snowman, guv? In Lunnon? You've gotter be joking!'

'It's all right,' said the Doctor. 'They're not due for another year or two. I was just having one of my bad-memory

decided. They were being a bit too obvious for that.

Two girls sat on stools by the bar, wearing baggy blouses and amazingly short skirts. One wasn't very pretty, but the other had a frizz of ginger hair, a warm, freckled complexion and good legs. Fitz caught her eye, and to his amazement she smiled at him, and straightaway got up and walked over to their table.

Then he realised that she was a waitress.

'Liberation for the masses,' murmured Sam, close to Fitz's ear. 'And the servants are all women, and they have to show their legs. I'm beginning to work out what was wrong with the sixties.'

Fitz frowned at her, but before he could reply the Doctor had started – as usual – on a completely different subject. 'I was in Havana for Castro's funeral, you know. They all loved him again by then.'

Fitz decided to ignore this sociopolitical chitchat and general name-dropping. Instead he smiled again at the waitress. She returned the smile, flicking her hair back from her face.

'Three coffees, please,' said the Doctor abstractedly. His eyes were on the café entrance.

Fitz turned back to the waitress, but she was on her way to the back of the café, where she vanished through a doorway that had no door, but was instead hung with streamers of coloured plastic. The streamers clattered and tangled as she walked through.

'So where's Rex?' Sam was asking.

'Not here yet,' replied the Doctor. 'But he will be. Every Thursday night, eight o'clock. He was very punctual, for an anarchist.'

Fitz was startled. Anarchist? 'Who is this Rex? Is he a real anarchist?'

'Oh, not just that: Jean-Pierre Rex is the King of the Anarchists. At least that's what they call him. It's an absurd title, a contradiction in terms. Like the man – ah, here he is.'

Fitz turned, expecting a commotion – or perhaps the scene from the gangster movie where the Big Boss comes in and everyone falls silent. Instead, he saw a small man wearing a leather trench coat and a beret shaking the rain from his umbrella before folding it neatly and putting it in the hat stand by the door. Nobody was taking any notice of him. His hair was black, worn long around his shoulders, his face round with a dark moustache. He looked like a cross between the Liquorice Allsort Man and Che Guevara. Fitz decided that the latter was probably intentional, the former unavoidable.

Rex walked to a table in the corner from where a dirty plate and an empty cup had not yet been collected by the waitress, and sat down. After a moment he pulled a paperback book from his pocket and began reading. Fitz saw the familiar blue-and-white jacket of a Pelican book: fact, then, not fiction.

'How do we get to meet him?' asked Sam.

'I don't know,' said the Doctor. 'How about...' He frowned, then smiled brightly. 'How about we go up to him and say hello?'

He stood up and walked across to the man, Sam in his wake. Fitz hesitated, then decided to stay at the table. He wasn't sure about meeting an anarchist. This was a Doctor-and-Sam thing: they hadn't told him about the game they were playing, so he wasn't going to join in.

'Three coffees, sir?'

Fitz looked up, saw the waitress with a red tray bearing three steaming cups. 'Thanks,' he said. He leaned close to her ear as she put the drinks on the table. 'They've just got up to consult the King of the Anarchists on matters of state.' He winked, inclined his head to the corner table. The Doctor was shaking hands with Jean-Pierre Rex, gesturing at Sam.

The waitress glanced over, nodded, started to walk away.

'Hey!' said Fitz, but she was gone, vanished through the doorway to the kitchen with its multicoloured plastic streamers.

Surely it hadn't been *that* bad a joke? She didn't seem to have been listening. Perhaps she was tired, or just too used to customers trying to chat her up. What had Sam said? 'Don't assume every woman's life centres around getting a man.' Well, in her time, maybe not. But right here and now... Fitz looked down at his silk shirt, his white jacket and trousers, his leather shoes. He was younger and better dressed than any of the other men in here, *including* the King of the Anarchists. The waitress ought to at least look at him, if only out of curiosity.

But, thinking about it, she hadn't seemed to notice the Doctor in his Edwardian get-up, or Sam with her short hair, jeans and nineties sweatshirt.

Fitz frowned, looked back at Sam and the Doctor talking to Rex. None of the other diners were looking at them. It was as if they weren't quite visible, as if they existed in a space fractionally turned aside from reality. He remembered the way that everyone on the Vega space station had spoken English, remembered the Doctor's muttered explanation about the TARDIS and her telepathic circuits. Perhaps the

TARDIS could do more than translate: perhaps it could alter perceptions, perform mental conjuring tricks that made its inhabitants invisible except when they wanted to be seen. Hadn't the Doctor said something about a 'chameleon circuit'? Fitz remembered the TARDIS parked outside Earl's Court station, and wondered what would happen if a passer-by tried to use it as a police box. Would they see the vast brass cathedral of the console room? Or a little black plastic phone, with the friendly voice of a London bobby on the end of it?

Fitz shivered. The Doctor had never *explained* the TARDIS. Sam didn't seem to care. Fitz decided that he would have to find out more, somehow. Sometime.

He became aware of the café again, the smell of garlic and coffee, the red neon sign in the window. Rex, the Doctor and Sam were walking back to his table, the Doctor talking, Rex nodding, Sam with her hands in her pockets.

Then Rex was towering over him, taller than he had seemed, or maybe just somehow *bigger.* His eyes locked on to Fitz's, field guns finding their range and target. 'I hear you have your own country. The Fitz Free State, no?'

Fitz swallowed, wondered if he was serious. What *had* the Doctor told him?

'I can sing my National Anthem if you like,' he said. But as a riposte, the line sounded feeble. In any case, Rex appeared not to have heard: he was calling the waitress, who had reappeared from behind the plastic streamers as if by magic. She came to the table, and Rex put a hand on her arm. 'Red wine,' he said. 'And glasses for my friends.'

Then his field-gun gaze returned to Fitz. 'Even in the country of your own mind, you must have a state of constant revolution,' he said. 'Nothing can remain the same, year to year, even day to day. That's the road to ossification of the brain. Anarchy is about freeing the mind from the instructions of history as much as freeing the body from the institutions of state. Sometimes I find it hard to make people understand that.'

'I'm sure –' Fitz began, but Rex just went on talking.

'Of course it isn't easy to maintain this state of flux, this attitude that any change is good. It is too easy to become… comfortable.' He made the word sound obscene. 'Too easy to forget that in comfort there is always oppression, oppression of the self, oppression of others. *Always*. You understand this?'

'Yes, but –'

'And therefore even in your own country, the country of your mind, you must stage the Revolution. Every day, every hour, every minute. Yes?'

Fitz began to feel dizzy under the barrage of words. He looked helplessly at the Doctor, who was cradling his coffee cup in his hands as if it were a kitten. The Doctor only shrugged and said, 'I must say it's a very nice Havana blend, though of course it doesn't come from Havana.'

'It comes from the oppressed workers of Brazil,' snapped Rex. 'Workers who get up at five in the morning and work twelve hours in the plantations, or in the factories where they prepare the beans and make up the extracts. Workers who have no rights, no union, no meaningful vote, and who are paid less in a week than it costs to buy a single cup of coffee here. I have ordered wine. It is still made by oppressed workers, but at least they are not starving.'

During this speech the artillery of his gaze moved from Fitz to the Doctor, which allowed Fitz to notice Sam, who was staring at the anarchist goggle-eyed, as if she were a Christian and he an accredited representative of God.

Fitz felt his sense of humour returning. He stood up again and signalled to the waitress, who had reappeared with a bottle of wine and a handful of glasses. 'Three more oppressive espressos, please. And make sure you don't give us a bill, because all the money goes to exploitative industrialists.'

He saw Sam looking at him appalled, but to his surprise Rex laughed. 'That's right, don't take my word. Find it out for yourself.' A huge hand grabbed Fitz's arm, and Fitz felt the guns open up again. 'But when you do, you won't think it's so funny any more. Do you know, there is a place in Colombia where there is an emerald mine, and children live in the dirt at the bottom of the slurry that comes out of the mine? They look for emeralds that the miners missed. Very, very rarely, they find one. Most of them make up their living by selling their bodies to tourists. *Children.*'

Fitz sat down. Somewhere behind him, the coffee machine roared. He looked at the Doctor, who was sipping from his cup. 'Is that true?'

'Very probably. Or something like it. The universe is full of evil places.'

'But it doesn't have to be!' declaimed Rex. 'If we can liberate ourselves from the habits imposed by oppressive institutions, if we can learn to think in a better way –'

'It gets better,' said Sam. 'But you're right, the revolution must be continuous, or it doesn't work. People get lazy again.'

Fitz saw Rex focus on Sam. To his amazement, he reached

out and patted her hand. 'You are an intelligent woman!' he exclaimed. 'Are you perhaps a librarian? Most of the intelligent women I meet are librarians. You should wear your hair long, and have glasses with thick rims, no?'

Fitz noticed that Rex's entire manner had changed: the field artillery had gone, replaced by a flirtatious bonhomie. He was a different person.

But Sam didn't seem fazed. 'I reckon I'm a revolutionary, like you,' she said. 'I just use different methods, that's all.'

'And what methods are those?'

Rex's voice was suggestive, and Fitz wondered if Sam would take offence. But if she did, she didn't show it. She just took a sip of her coffee and met his eyes quietly. 'Peaceful ones.'

Rex shook his head slowly. 'In truth, there are no peaceful methods. Only violence succeeds.'

'That's not true!'

'You are a woman. Naturally you would think –'

'Why should my gender make a difference? How many revolutions have you been in lately? I've been in two – no, three. And a couple of rather nasty wars, and some protests. I never saw any incident where the violent solution was the best one.'

A short silence. The Doctor sipped his coffee, his eyes on the two men in red shirts, who were talking loudly in Spanish. The waitress served the wine. Her arm touched Fitz's shoulder as she filled his glass. He looked up at her and winked. She stared at him for a moment, then frowned and hurried off behind her screen of plastic streamers, leaving Fitz with the memory of a pale, abstracted face and eyes a very pretty shade of green.

Damn. She probably had a boyfriend. Perhaps he was the owner. Perhaps he had a bad temper.

'I was in Algeria,' said Rex suddenly. 'In the army. I deserted after one year. After what I saw they were doing...' He shook his head. 'You cannot understand.'

'Try me.' Sam's eyes were fixed on Rex's.

But Rex just took a gulp of wine. 'You haven't been in the front line.'

'I have.'

'But you haven't killed anyone.'

'I have.'

The Doctor's face crumpled for an instant, as if in pain. Was he surprised? Fitz was, but tried not to show it.

Rex had started to laugh, a long, masculine, thigh-slapping guffaw. A heavy hand clapped down on Fitz's shoulder. 'She is a good bluffer, this young woman, eh? I would not like to gamble at cards with her!'

Yes. Of course. Sam was bluffing. That was the obvious explanation, wasn't it? Fitz couldn't believe how relieved he felt. He glanced at the Doctor, but he was busy with the Spanish conversation again, or perhaps he was reading the posters on the walls.

'I'd really looked forward to meeting you,' said Sam suddenly. 'I've read *The Anarchy of the Future* and *The Liberated Mind*. I thought you had a lot of interesting things to say. I thought you were ahead of your time. Now I'm not so sure.'

'Ahead of my time? What is time but an illusion? The Revolution is continuous, all points on the cycle are the same. The things I have said and done happened a hundred years ago, and they will happen again a thousand years in the future. I am not a Marxist, who believes in the inevitability of progress. I know that nothing changes, in the end.'

'That doesn't mean you shouldn't try.' The Doctor was back from wherever he'd been hiding inside his mind. His hand was on Rex's arm, his gaze on the man's face. 'We all have to do what we can to make the world a better place. Try, try and try again.'

'Maybe,' said Rex. 'It is the quality of "what we can" that makes the difference, I think. Marx would argue that this is dictated by our position in society, but I think it is possible for the mind itself to be liberated –'

Fitz took another gulp of wine. He could feel the conversation slipping out of his focus, to some place where politics and dialectic were the only thing that existed, and the real world was a blurred dream floating a long way below. He stood up, muttered an excuse-me and headed for the kitchen doorway. The red-haired waitress was coming out, a tray of food in each hand. Fitz silently applauded his own good timing.

'Uh – the gents?' he said.

She inclined her head to the left. Her lips curled in a smile. They were soft, and thin: she didn't seem to be wearing lipstick.

'Are you –' He glanced at the kitchen doorway, the chef, the possible boyfriend. 'Are you doing anything after work?'

The smile curled up a bit more. 'Walking home,' she said. Then: 'Excuse me.'

'Of course.'

When he came out, she was waiting by the coffee machine. The smile was still there.

'Did you really want three more espressos?'

Fitz frowned, then remembered his little joke. He smiled. 'I could do with them. To wake me up.' He nodded at the table. The Doctor was waving a fork near Rex's face. His hair was a halo again, tinged red by the neon light from the window. Surprisingly, he was drinking his wine.

'Marxist-anarchist dialectic isn't my strong point,' Fitz told the woman, meeting her eyes.

She shook her head. 'Nor mine. I only work here because my mother won't give me any money. Which is in turn because my man's a "pop singer". As she likes to call it.' She flicked her hair back from her face.

'Your man?' Fitz tried very hard not to sound disappointed, but knew he hadn't succeeded.

She laughed, to let him know she'd seen through him. But it was a gentle laugh: she wasn't making fun of him. 'Yes. He's Ed Hill, the singer in Kathmandu.'

'If he's in Kathmandu, what are you doing here?' asked Fitz, as innocently as possible.

She laughed again. 'OK, baby. For that one you can walk me home.' The sharp American twang took Fitz by surprise: she was good at it. Returning to her own British middle-class accent, she added, 'But just remember – Ed's not really in Kathmandu, he's in Shooters Hill, and if you try anything he'll thump you.'

Fitz decided to prove that she wasn't the only one who could do an accent. He saluted sharply, clicked his heels together, said, 'You haf my verd as a German officer!'

'And you have nearly an hour to wait. Enrico goes mad if I don't clear up properly and we're not even closed yet.'

Fitz glanced at the table. The Doctor and Rex were

swigging wine, talking loudly; Sam was watching their conversation as if it were a tennis match. 'It's going to be a long hour,' he said.

'You'll survive.'

'– the power to change things. The power of words, the power of fists, is there any difference?'

'As Wittgenstein said –'

Fitz sighed, and made his way back to his seat.

The Greeks had been right, thought Sam, looking at the statue of Eros perched in the middle of Piccadilly Circus. Heroes were imperfect, and even gods weren't faultless. There might be perfect individuals who rose above human frailties, but they lived only in the imagination. Real-life heroes were different.

Jean-Pierre Rex might be the greatest anarchist thinker of his generation: his work might right now be encouraging thousands of young people who wouldn't otherwise have thought to experiment with the concept of 'no nation, no race, no flag'. He had influenced the lives of millions – but Sam could still feel the touch of his hand on her backside. He'd done it as they'd left the café. She'd glared him down, but he'd only grinned at her. The patronising, sexist… She shook her head slowly. Perhaps she could make him believe that women were people too, by the end of the evening. Her own little contribution to the history of the sixties, and the liberation of the mind.

The Doctor and Rex were walking ahead, hands in pockets, presumably discussing the future of the universe. Fragments of philosophy and dialectic occasionally broke through the growl of car engines. The rain had stopped, and the sky above was dark, empty of clouds. If there were stars, they were drowned in the glare of neon lights. Sam was walking alone – Fitz was gone, grinning hugely and making far too obvious gestures at the red-headed waitress he'd been ogling all night. The idiot.

In a way she was glad that he was gone – it made things easier. If anything came up, she and the Doctor could do a number 47 escape manoeuvre without worrying that they might lose Fitz. Or they could plan a number 5 without Fitz wondering what they were talking about and getting angry because he was being left out. She could understand how he felt, up to a point – travelling with the Doctor was a bewildering and unsettling experience. But she could remember those first heady days, four years ago in her lifetime, when they'd defeated vampires in LA and Tractites in alternative worlds, when everything had seemed like a miracle. Why didn't Fitz feel the excitement? He'd seemed to, at first, but now he was edgy, as if he wasn't quite sure he'd made the right decision.

Well, if he was going to go, this was the best time period to do so. It was near enough to his own. But Sam wasn't sure she wanted him to: travelling with the Doctor for a long time reminded you how much you missed purely human company. And Fitz wasn't so bad: he was funny, he was intelligent, and he wasn't as deeply cynical as he made himself out to be. He wasn't even all that sexist, considering the time in which he'd been brought up.

What had the Doctor said, back in the TARDIS? 'If he knew, it could make things worse'? Obviously the Doctor too had sensed Fitz's edginess. They would have to talk about it sometime – or, better still, she should talk to Fitz.

In the meantime, there was the problem of the Revolution Man. She glared ahead at Jean-Pierre Rex again, and wondered when the Doctor would ask him. She'd suggested the man as a contact, and was beginning to deeply regret it. She'd lost an idol, and she was pretty sure he'd be no help. He sounded impractical, idealistic; any serious activists were bound to keep their distance from him.

Suddenly the Doctor glanced back at her sharply, flicked his eyebrows in a familiar coded gesture. She saw that Rex was glaring at the Doctor, his face flushed dark with blood.

Ah. Obviously the Doctor, too, had decided that it was time to start the business of the evening.

'How dare you?' snapped Rex. 'What do you think I am, a traitor? If I knew I wouldn't tell you!'

The Doctor put a hand on the shorter man's shoulder. Sam heard his soothing voice, saw his smile, heard a phrase: 'The safety of the world –'

'Don't give me that mind-control nonsense!' Rex was shouting now. 'I don't believe in it! The mind is free – it must be free. If people don't believe in that there's no point at all!'

Several passers-by were staring now. Another bus rumbled past, slowing for the circus. Suddenly Rex had moved, and the Doctor was on his knees on the pavement, an expression of astonishment on his face.

Sam saw Rex on the platform of the bus, hurrying up the stairs. She started to run after him, but the bus was pulling away into the traffic. Horns blared as she moved out into the road. She stepped back to the pavement, turned to check on the Doctor. He was standing, with his hands spread wide.

'I told him,' he said. 'The world is in danger. I *told* him.'

'Not everyone listens,' Sam pointed out. 'And not everyone

believes everything you tell them. He probably thought you were nuts.' She looked after the bus, now turning the corner towards Trafalgar Square, and added more seriously, 'Do you think he's the one?'

'Probably not. But he knows something about it, that's obvious.'

'Or he thought you were an undercover cop. Just because he has things to hide –'

'– it doesn't mean that he's hiding what we're trying to find.' The Doctor smiled at her. 'Quite right.' He looked around anxiously for a moment, then said, 'Television.' Sam raised her eyebrows. 'We need to find the next incident. It should be today. The best place to look will be on TV. The ITN news, I think.'

Sam knew better than to argue.

'We'd better tell Fitz where we're going,' she said.

'Oh, we won't need to,' said the Doctor airily.

'I'm definitely going to have to talk to you about Fitz,' muttered Sam.

The Doctor ignored her, but she knew he'd heard.

Chapter Three

Everybody was expecting a fight.

Paolo could see the men and women placed at strategic points – crouching behind walls, behind the overturned cars, one in a tree. He could see the glint of bottles in their hands. The marchers in the centre of the road were nervous, their crude red-painted banners wavering. Their footsteps echoed off the white buildings, the Roman stone. The sunlight was bright, too bright, bleaching garlanded balconies and low gardens with its glare, casting thick shadows. Some of the shadows held dim faces, watchful eyes.

Antonio was right. Their salaries didn't cover this. They should be on strike themselves, not wearing the gold-buttoned blue uniform of the *Polizia*, batons ready, and pistols, yes, pistols in their holsters with live ammunition. In the name of God, did Captain Lopresti think they were going to shoot these people?

He glanced at Antonio, next to him in the line. His friend's narrow face was framed by a short, pointed, golden beard; his gaze was concentrated, as ever, forward, directly ahead at the problem to be solved next. Paolo preferred to think ahead, to go around the immediate problem to the root cause, the primary motive. They were a good team.

'Greed,' he whispered to Antonio. 'That's what started all this. The bosses want all the money, the workers want more than they have now. Something has to give, one side or the other.'

Antonio nodded. 'Watch the corner, by the Alassio. There's a bunch of them there.'

Paolo looked, saw half a dozen students sitting on the tables of the street café, skinny in their American blue jeans. Why did they think that everything American was good, when most of them were communists? It was only skin-deep, all of it. So stupid of them to be violent, over something that meant so little. He imagined that, in a few years' time, most of them would be raising families in the suburbs, political fervour forgotten in the shrieking of the children and the need to keep bread and olives on the table.

If they got the chance. If no one in the police lines lost their head and started shooting.

The demonstrators were quite close now, and had stopped their march, the column crumpling into an irregular front that was already spilling out over walls and into the low gardens of the houses and hotels that lined the street. Shouts were getting louder, angrier.

'Draw batons!'

Paolo and Antonio glanced at each other in near disbelief. Captain Lopresti's voice was eager – stupidly eager, as usual. Did he think that medals would be won for this action? Reluctantly, Paolo drew the shiny black stick from its holster. It felt too weighty, too dangerous.

The police lines were starting to move, a ragged advance for which no one had exactly given an order. Paolo's uniform felt heavy and hot as he and Antonio stepped forward. Antonio quickly took the lead, slipping around the edge of the relatively harmless placard-wavers and towards the students in the café, who were already standing on the tables and shouting. With growing alarm, Paolo noticed that some had stones in their hands – crude, heavy chunks, most probably scavenged from the site of the old Hotel Imperial.

Antonio glanced round, winked. 'If they try to pitch those boulders they'll end up with squashed toes!'

Maybe, thought Paolo. But if they do hit anyone, it could be serious. 'They should give us crash helmets like the French, not these ridiculous caps,' he said.

'Don't worry!' said Antonio, still advancing.

The young men began to jeer. '*Fascisti! Fascisti!*'

'Don't be stupid!' shouted Antonio. 'Just clear the street and there won't be any trouble!'

A rock crashed to the ground near his feet. Paolo realised that the stuff was concrete, hollow tubes of the stuff. It was easy to throw –

A piece cracked down on the pavement beside him and split open. Paolo saw something inside, and dived away just as the tube shattered, sending a puff of flame into the air, and shrapnel in all directions.

He felt impacts on his uniform, smelled scorched cloth.

Ahead of him, Antonio was yelling, stamping his feet on the ground, batting at leg with his hands. Paolo stared for a moment, then saw the smoke, and the lick of flame, almost invisible in the bright sunlight.

'Roll!' he yelled. At the same time he took off his own jacket, the action almost a reflex, an echo of training. But he'd never done this for real.

Antonio was on fire.

He was rolling now, still yelling. There was much more smoke. He could hear the students jeering – but one shouting, 'That was stupid, Marco!'

No time for them. He looked at Antonio, saw that most of

the smoke was coming from the lower part of his legs. Good – that was easy. He lifted his friend's legs, wrapped the jacket around the flames.

Antonio gave a shudder of pain. Smoke leaked out from the jacket.

'How bad is it?' asked Paolo, but before his friend could answer Paolo felt a hand shove him between the shoulder blades. Caught unprepared, he sprawled over Antonio's body.

Furious, Paolo turned around, saw the students pounding along the road. The motions of their legs seemed curiously slow. Someone was screaming obscenities. After a moment, Paolo became aware of his own raw throat and realised that he was the one shouting.

Control yourself, he thought. He stood up, and discovered he no longer had his baton. He couldn't see it on the ground: one of the students must have it. He ran after them, shouting again. He could see other police ahead, scuffles, a young woman in pink being hit over the head.

Curse Lopresti. This wasn't going to work. He could see the cameras of RAI, the Italian television service, a flash reporter in his expensive suit, everything rolling on to film. The woman was screaming, blood running down her face. On the evening news the police would be pigs, oppressors.

Perhaps I should give up this job, thought Paolo. It isn't right for a family man.

He stood there, uncertain, in the middle of the wide pavement. Feet clattered on stone around him; there were shouts; there was even something that sounded like a gunshot. It seemed distant, not quite part of the scene, like the soundtrack to a programme playing on a neighbour's TV.

Paolo saw a space on a wall, and sat down on it, his head in his hands. His forehead was slick with sweat.

A hand wrenched at his body, hard, ripping at muscles. Paolo winced, jumped up.

No one was there.

'Hey! Paolo! We need you over here!'

But Paolo couldn't move. Something was holding his body, pressing on it, squeezing the air out of his lungs and his blood to his face.

A heart attack, he thought. But it can't be. I'm only thirty-one.

Then he was moving, his feet dragging on the ground, his body twisting this way and that. Several people looked up and stared.

Another wrenching pain in his chest, and he was on the ground. His gun clattered on the pavement. How had it been torn loose? He looked down, saw the holster flapping open, the leather torn.

The gun was scraping along the pavement. On its own.

Paolo stared. It was like a scene from a Disney movie. The gun was moving, like a leaf in the wind. All his senses were sharp again, the scene clear. The protesters were clumped together, the students were throwing their lumps of concrete and improvised petrol bombs. The police were retreating. The air was full of smoke and shouting.

It was all real, and the gun was still moving.

Suddenly it jumped into the air, wavering, jumping up and down a little. Paolo almost laughed – it looked so ridiculous, like a metal bird in a clumsy flight.

It was flying towards Antonio, who was sitting up, his face pale, unwrapping the jacket from his legs.

The gun snuggled against Antonio's scalp.

Paolo cried out at the very moment that it fired.

He ran then, ran *away*, and the crowd were growing quiet, staring, wondering, and they even made way for him and somehow he knew it was behind him, the gun, the metal bird, and *what had he done to deserve this*?

He felt the first bullet as a shove in the back, a thump that knocked the breath from him and left him sprawling.

He didn't feel the second bullet at all.

'So,' said Sam slowly, 'How many telekinetic races do we know?'

On the black-and-white TV, the tiny, blurred image of the gun flying through the air was frozen. The commentator was talking about a 'freak incident'.

'Or maybe people with access to invisibility technology.' The Doctor hadn't taken his eyes from the screen. His face had its 'serious look' – a downward curl of the lips, a hollowness about the eyes. He was far away from Sam, only a fraction of his mind on their conversation.

The news had moved on to another item. The grainy picture irritated Sam's eyes: she wanted it to be sharp, real. It looked artificial, a caricature image. There was no one else in the small hotel sitting room, only empty chairs and faded wallpaper. She got up and turned off the TV. The switch made a solid click, and the picture took a full three seconds to shrink away to a dot afterwards.

'All that wasted energy,' she muttered, though she knew that far more would be wasted in her own time.

The Doctor didn't reply, a sure sign that he was barely listening.

'I'll give you some cash – get a flight to Rome,' he said. 'Tomorrow morning, as early as you can. Look around, see what you can find. Take this.' He was fishing around in his pockets – now he produced a small, jewelled brooch.

'It's not my style,' protested Sam. 'And wouldn't it be easier to go in the TARDIS?'

The Doctor shrugged, smiled his smile. 'The TARDIS has to stay here,' he said. He didn't say why, and Sam knew better than to argue. 'When the brooch beeps at you, have a look at the reading. If it's higher than one hundred, get out.'

'What's it measuring, exactly?'

'Spatial distortion. Which is the only thing I know of that makes trees blow around in a wind that isn't there.'

Sam glanced at the TV. She had noticed the trees moving, hadn't thought about the wind. She wondered how the Doctor managed it – always observing everything, always drawing the right conclusions.

Well, nearly always right.

'I'd better pack,' she said.

The Doctor nodded, still abstracted.

Sam left the sitting room, walked up creaky stairs to the small box room where she'd put her hastily packed overnight bag. It had the same cheap wallpaper as the sitting room, and a slightly damp smell.

Why they couldn't have stayed in the TARDIS, she didn't know. The Doctor had been a bit cagey – he'd said the old girl needed a rest. It wasn't just Fitz who was being kept in the dark, she decided. She sniffed the air in the room once again, then made a decision.

The Doctor was still in the sitting room. The TV was on again, and a small child in a bright-red jumper was playing a board game with the Doctor. Garish yellow card, tokens in several colours. The legend CHINESE CHEQUERS ran in red, burning letters across the centre of the board.

'I'll have the cash now,' said Sam quietly, when she'd got the Doctor's attention. 'And fly overnight.'

Did the Doctor's expression carry the faint trace of a frown?

But all he did was reach into his pocket and give her an old-fashioned leather purse, as unsuitable as the brooch.

'Try it your way, then,' he said. 'It might work.'

As if she had a plan.

'I just don't fancy that room.'

But the Doctor didn't reply. His eyes were on the board, concentrating on his next move.

Fitz woke up with a sore neck. He was on a strange couch, in a strange room that smelled of old wine and stale smoke.

Nothing new in that. Nothing new, either, in the dull feeling in his skull, which meant too much wine, and the rasp in his throat, which meant too many cigarettes. Hadn't he been going to give up? Sam had told him –

Sam. The TARDIS. Time travel.

Nineteen sixty-seven.

He took in the bright colours on the walls, the square of copper-coloured sunlight drifting between a swirl of enigmatic purples and a stark outline of a man's face. The man had long hair, a pointed beard and heavy eyebrows. His expression was enigmatic. Somebody had painted crude flowers in his hair and above his head, a stark, ineffective contrast.

Fitz got up, winced, rubbed his neck and padded across the

room. He found his shoes, mixed in a pile of other shoes by the door. They were wet and slightly muddy. They'd crossed Blackheath, in a light drizzle. Talking, talking, talking. The future of the world. The meaning of anarchy, of love, of truth. Fitz had loved it, had loved the sound of her voice, the innocent intelligence in her mind. She was his sort of girl, no doubt of that.

Shame about the 'man'.

Fitz hadn't liked him from the minute he'd seen the house. He hadn't actually seen Ed: the rock star was getting his beauty sleep. They'd finished a bottle of wine and a packet of cigarettes, then Maddie had quietly gone up to share Ed's bed, leaving Fitz with the couch and a blanket.

In the morning light, the flat looked even more garish. The walls were draped with hangings in colours too bright to be comfortable, some printed with the face of a long-haired, crudely smiling bloke – Fitz had a feeling that this was Ed.

How *could* someone as intelligent as Maddie fall for –

Fitz shrugged. These things happened. He went through an unpainted wooden door into what seemed to be a kitchen – at any rate, there was a stove there, with a shiny new kettle on it. There didn't, however, seem to be a fridge, nor any food. He saw another doorway, filled with plastic streamers like the ones in the restaurant. After walking through, he found a fridge, another cooker, and a stone sink. There was a small radio on top of the fridge.

Footsteps descended the stairs. Heavy, boot-clad steps – surely not Maddie's. The steps crossed the room behind him, a body clattered through the plastic hangings.

'Hi! I'm Ed.'

Fitz turned, saw a face only slightly more real than the

version on the prints, and with the same crude smile.

'You're in Kathmandu, aren't you?' Maddie hadn't talked much about the band last night, but Fitz had gathered that they were hot property, with several records in the charts. Ed was probably big-headed, self-centred: best to show an interest.

But Ed only nodded. 'And you're a scientist.'

Fitz's surprise must have shown in his face, because Ed laughed. 'I'm more of a philosopher,' said Fitz.

Ed nodded again. Fitz noticed that his eyes weren't focusing, but instead wandered slowly from object to object, as if half in a dream.

'"I think, therefore I am".' Ed shook his head. His face was wide and bullish, his lips thin. He no longer looked like the star on the print. 'No, man, you think too much. You should ball more.'

'Ed?' Maddie's voice.

'He should ball more!' Ed grabbed Fitz's arms, the touch soft yet aggressive. 'You should have done it last night, out on the common like rabbits. Perhaps you did, man. Hey, I wouldn't mind. She's a pretty lady.' His breath stank of garlicky spices.

Ed's heavy body had Fitz almost trapped against the fridge. He wondered whether he should hit him, or try one of the escape manoeuvres he and Sam had practised.

The plastic streamers rattled and Maddie walked through, in a long dressing-gown.

'Ed! Come on, stop it now. You're frightening poor Fitz.'

Ed grunted, but turned away. He gave Fitz a lewd wink, muttered, 'Freedom of the planet, man, freedom of the planet.'

Maddie and Fitz stared at each other, then Maddie laughed, just a little nervously. 'He's OK. He just had a bad trip.' She shrugged. 'You know.'

'Trip?'

'Acid.' She frowned. 'Oh, you don't know. You are a bit out of it, aren't you? OK, it's a new thing. Makes you see the world… differently. It's great, normally. But some of it isn't made properly. Ed calls it "devil drops" when that happens.' She lowered her eyes. 'It's great, normally,' she repeated.

Fitz remembered Ed's heavy face and decided to reserve judgement.

They had breakfast in the living room, with trays on their laps. Maddie had fried some eggs and bacon, and served fresh coffee from a silver percolator. Fitz decided that Top Thirty hits had their advantages.

'Smoke?' Maddie thrust a pack of Marlboros at him.

He shook his head. 'I'm trying to give it up.'

'You weren't last night!'

'It's bad for you.'

It didn't seem convincing, somehow. Sam's lectures on tar and lung cancer seemed to have vanished, become anachronistic.

'I think it's all a conspiracy,' said Maddie. 'A way to stop young people having fun.'

Fitz glanced at her. She was serious. But *was* it fun to smoke?

He stared at the packet, shook his head. Of course it wasn't fun. But nonetheless he helped himself to one, and lit it at the stove.

Maddie grinned.

Then she stared at him, and spoke in a quiet, level tone. 'What would you say about a drug that gave you the power to bend reality?'

Fitz shrugged. 'You mean…' He gestured upward, at the sleeping-it-off Ed.

She shook her head. 'I mean for real.'

Fitz picked up the coffee cup and stared at it for a moment. It was white, with an elaborate gold pattern on it: Aries the Ram.

'I mean, if you could change things, pick up that chair over there without touching it.'

'You mean telekinesis?' he asked.

'I don't know what I mean. But what if it happened?'

Fitz glanced up at her. Her eyes were fixed on his face. He remembered what Ed had said about his being a scientist, remembered that he'd thrown Maddie a line about being part of a scientific expedition. Why had he said that? Probably to cover up something he'd said about the Canvine on Vega.

He decided that he was going to have to drink less if he was going to stay with the Doctor.

'What drug is this?' he asked.

Maddie lowered her eyes. 'Oh, the name wouldn't mean anything. And I'm not sure – I mean, what I really want to know is, if you did think you'd done this telekinesis, would it be an illusion?'

Fitz frowned. The Doctor had mentioned psi powers once, he was sure of that. And telekinesis was a psi power, wasn't it? That meant it was real.

'Not necessarily,' said Fitz carefully. 'There is such a thing as real telekinesis.'

Maddie's reaction was extraordinary. She took a sharp breath, looked away. Her face went pale, almost grey.

Fitz thought for a moment, then decided that the time had come to try out his impression of the Doctor.

He leaned forward, took both her hands. 'Maddie,' he said, 'you'll have to tell me everything you know about this.'

She looked down at the table, took a deep breath. 'Not here,' she said at last. 'Let's go for a walk.'

It was a dull morning. Rome appeared in snatches as the plane descended, fragments of a half-dark city emerging from a cotton wool of clouds, illuminated like pieces of jewellery in a box. Sam pressed her nose against the tiny window of the plane, trying hard to spot the Colosseum, the dome of St Peter's, or anything else that she recognised. She didn't have much luck.

When they touched down, bouncing a little on the tarmac, the airport looked small, oddly informal. A cluster of buildings, a cluster of primitive-looking flying machines, dull silver in the overcast light. When she got to the door, the air was warm, despite the rain.

She was halfway down the steps when she saw him. The square figure with the bulldog head and short grey hair was unmistakable. He must have got out ahead of her – she was amazed she hadn't noticed him on the plane.

Jean-Pierre Rex.

By the time she'd reached the bottom of the steps she'd made her decision. Immediately in front of her were an elderly couple, well dressed, both quite big people. She kept behind them across the tarmac and into the cover of the airport buildings, and kept an eye on Rex. Inside the building was a passport check, a baggage collection point, and a customs desk, divided into red and green sections. The passport check was unbelievably informal: a single bearded man in a small booth. Sam got lucky: Rex was in front of the elderly couple she was using as cover. She heard the clerk say something, and Rex spoke: 'Witold Tietze? It's half German, half Polish. And I'm French. Work that one out, eh?' The clerk laughed.

So he was travelling under a false name. Well, that was no surprise. It was useful to know what it was, though.

At the check, she handed over her own passport, one of the Doctor's many falsies, this one in the name of a Mrs Evelyn Smith. The photo seemed to be of her seventeen-year-old self, but it got her through.

At customs, Rex simply walked through the green channel. Sam followed. There was no cover any more, but he didn't look round as they walked through a neon-lit hall and out into a crowd of tourists, taxis, shouting couriers in the uniforms of various travel companies, and large, multicoloured coaches.

Almost at once, Sam realised that she'd lost Rex. He'd just vanished into the hustle.

'Damn,' she muttered. She pushed her way around in the crowd for a few minutes, looking, but he was shorter than everyone else. Perhaps he had noticed he was being followed, after all, and had dodged her deliberately.

Perhaps. Nothing for it but to carry on, and hope it was just a coincidence that he too was in Rome. Sam found a taxi queue and settled down to wait, trying not to choke on the oily fumes. She'd been there about thirty seconds when a hand grabbed her arm and twisted it behind her back.

'Miss Jones.' Rex's French accent, edgy with fear. 'So nice of you to follow me such a long way. Perhaps now you will put your peaceful ideals into practice. Yes?'

Chapter Four

Stupid, thought Sam. Obviously Rex had seen her in the airport, and waited for his opportunity.

Two tourists pushed past them, dressed in garish colours, with black leather boxes around their necks. Cameras, Sam realised. She heard a snatch of conversation: 'I couldn't believe St Peter's was so *big*.' Then Rex pulled her aside, out of the flow of people, and pushed her against the wall next to a metal box that dispensed chocolate.

'Well?' he asked. His face was flushed. Anger? Exertion? It could hardly be the heat. His moustache looked exaggerated, almost artificial. Sam wondered what he would do if she tried to pull it off.

'I didn't follow you,' Sam told him. 'The Doctor sent me to look into the business with the flying gun. You must have seen it on the news.'

'Ah, yes.' Rex loosened his grip on her arm. 'Psychic investigators, wasn't it? That was the rubbish your Doctor friend told me. I didn't believe it yesterday and I don't believe it now.'

'Well, it's true,' said Sam, as patiently as possible. 'You saw the news report? The gun?'

'Yes. A trick. A special weapon, perhaps, that went wrong and turned on its owners. Some might see it as poetic justice, but it is not a proof of psychic powers.'

'Still, we felt we should –'

A twist of her arm. 'And you should be on the next plane back to London.'

'Or you break my arm in public?' In fact Sam was fairly sure

53

she could break Rex's hold without undue fuss, but she didn't want an obvious scene any more than he did.

Rex let her go. 'OK, stay then. But if I see you anywhere near me again, I will take action. Direct action. You understand?'

You're bluffing, thought Sam. She still couldn't take him seriously, after his ridiculous attempt at a pass in London, and his escape on a number 9 bus. But she faked a nervousness she didn't feel, and agreed to keep away.

Rex stalked off into the crowd and hailed a taxi. She let him go, waited for a while by the chocolate machine. A small child appeared, put a coin in the slot, extracted a pale-coloured bar that said it was strawberry flavour.

Sam rubbed her arm, then reached into her pocket and looked at the address the Doctor had given her for the offices of the TV network RAI. She needed to look at the original film, find out who had taken it, talk to them.

She set off, whistling as she made her way back to the still-disorderly queue for the taxis.

They stood on the Greenwich Meridian, where the Doctor's friend George Airy had divided the world, and Maddie told Fitz how it had felt to kill three hundred people.

'You're sure that's what happened?'

'It was on the radio the next morning. It was in Kashmir. I looked on a map: it seemed like the right place. I just wondered –' She broke off, frowned. 'Perhaps it wasn't an illusion. Perhaps it was some kind of psychic resonance. You know, people died, and I felt it because of the drug. But I didn't *cause* it – that part was just my imagination. Could it have been like that?'

Her hand on Fitz's arm was painfully tight, and he knew how much she wanted her words to be true. But he had to be careful. If he said anything too glib, she might think he was making it up just to comfort her. So he thought for a moment, looked down the steep green reach of Greenwich Park to Wren's Naval College and the river. There was a bus making its way along the road in front of the building: Fitz made himself wait until it had traversed the full length of the college and turned left towards the river before he replied.

'Well, it's a good deal more possible than telekinesis,' he said. 'Of the two I'd say a resonance – a telepathic phenomenon – is more likely.' He was still doing his Doctor impersonation. He had no idea whether his facts were right, but he suspected that the Doctor was often in the same position. The important thing, surely, was to say what the person wanted to hear.

Maddie's grip on his arm slackened, then she let go altogether. 'Can you find out?' she asked. 'I mean, if I could get you a sample of Om– erm, of the drug.'

Fitz glanced at her. There was a slight drizzle falling, and tiny fragments of it glinted in her red hair. She looked, he thought, stunning. 'Get me a sample,' he said, 'And I'll perform an analysis at the lab.'

She smiled. 'OK,' she said. 'But we're going to have to steal it from Ed.'

'Best leave that to you then, Mata Hari.'

She giggled. 'I know where he keeps it. But it might be tricky.'

'Meet me here at… six o'clock?'

She nodded, then, to his surprise, leaned forward and kissed him lightly on the cheek. 'Bye.'

As she ran away towards the heath, Fitz was surprised to find that he was blushing.

The RAI building was impressive: white marble and fountains, huge plate-glass doors, an aluminium sculpture called *The Spirit of Knowledge* in several languages, which resembled a TV transmitter of the period, complete with rippling rings to represent radiating information. Sam looked at it for a minute or so, and decided that the artist hadn't quite got it, though she couldn't put her finger on what was wrong.

Inside, it was like stepping into the nineteenth century. There was a cool foyer with a high ceiling and a massive chandelier. Behind a huge, dark wooden desk sat a bemedalled commissionaire who looked as though he should be working for the Ritz. He solemnly examined the letter of introduction the Doctor had provided. The organisation it purported to be from didn't quite exist yet, and the Brigadier who'd signed it was still a colonel in the British Army, but Sam hoped that it looked impressive enough.

To her relief, it worked. The man didn't even ask any further questions, just nodded her through and gave her a door number, 3133. 'Signor Catelli,' he called after her. 'That's his name.'

There was a lift, an open cage of black iron. Sam could see the stone of the floors as it passed through them, the metal of doors, and grilled windows that showed long, brightly lit corridors. On the third floor, she had to ask directions twice before she found office 3133. The fittings here were very different from the grand lobby: a brown plasticky substance on the floors, loose chipboard walls painted dove-grey. Here and there a heavy old door or a piece of carved plaster reflected the building's original grandeur, but everything seemed to have been either knocked in or knocked out. Red lights flashed above darkened doors. Cables snaked across passageways. People ran up and down, shouting, carrying briefcases, or wheeling trolleys full of chunky metallic equipment.

At last she found Catelli, standing in the doorway of his office, talking to a young woman. He wore an orange suit and a purple tie, and his thick black hair framed his face with sideburns and a short beard. He read her letter of introduction, nodded briskly and dismissed the woman, then invited Sam in. The office was tiny and hot, with plasterboard walls and only half a window. It smelled of cigarettes. Catelli lit one, offered her one. Sam shook her head.

'I was there,' he said, indicating the letter. 'I saw the gun move by itself. A special weapon, is it?'

Sam shrugged. 'That's what we're trying to find out.'

Catelli laughed. 'The world is changing, that's for sure. But I don't think your people control it. Nor your so-called enemies in Russia.' He preened his hair for a moment with a hand. 'I think they know that. Why else send a girl?'

He seemed oblivious to the insulting nature of his remark. Sam decided that it was pointless being defensive: she'd begun to understand the meaning of the phrase 'institutionalised sexism' in a way they'd never taught her at school.

'So – what do you think?' she asked.

He steepled his hands on the desk. 'I think that there is a

new spirit to things,' he said slowly. 'A spirit of liberty. Freedom to think. Freedom to change things. Freedom to see things in the way you choose. Freedom to make love to anyone you like.' Sam noticed that his eyes had strayed to the level of her waist.

Oh, no, not again, she thought. Is this all they think about in 1967? She tried to look severe, but it didn't seem to affect Catelli.

'I think that sometimes that spirit… manifests itself, yes?'

'This "spirit" killed two people, signor,' said Sam.

He had the grace to look embarrassed. He stood up suddenly, stubbed out his cigarette. 'Come on, I will show you the place. You will feel it too. And there is… something else.'

His hand patted her backside as they left the room, and he winked at her.

'I'd rather you didn't do that,' she said.

He frowned, and Sam realised that he hadn't even noticed what he'd done, and that it certainly wasn't related to whatever he'd been talking about. Just to keep things clear, she kept well ahead of him until she reached the lift. Nineteen sixty-seven, she decided, was going to be hard work.

Fitz looked at the hotel where the Doctor had chosen to stay. Its four storeys were squeezed into a narrow brick façade between a fish-and-chip shop and a greengrocer's. Each shop had dilapidated-looking flats above it, with dusty windows and torn curtains. The hotel didn't look in much better order. Fitz decided that it was exactly the sort of flea pit he'd use himself. But in his case it would be because of lack of money. The Doctor never seemed to have a problem with that. Why on Earth had he chosen it?

Fitz had got to the TARDIS at Earl's Court only to find a notice, OUT OF ORDER, hanging on the door. After struggling to get in for a minute or so, Fitz had thought to turn the notice round. The name and address of the hotel had been on the back.

'The Alhambra,' he muttered. 'He'd better have a good excuse.'

He found the Doctor in the sitting room, earnestly discussing rabbits with a small girl and a shabby-looking middle-aged woman who might be her mother, or perhaps even her grandmother. It took some time for Fitz to break into the conversation, and even longer to get the subject away from chinchillas and rabbit breeds. At last the child and her guardian left, and Fitz could explain what had happened to Maddie and Ed.

The Doctor nodded. 'Yes, but the main thing is to find out who is making this stuff available. It certainly doesn't originate on Earth.'

'Maddie said she could get me a sample. She was worried.'

'Yes, yes, she would be. She must be going mad with guilt if she really believes she's done it. But what we need to know is: who's using it to deliberately kill people, and why? And why they're letting everyone else use it too.'

Fitz felt as if he'd been kicked.

'You think it is telekinesis then? Maddie hoped –'

'Oh, yes, I'm sure it's genuine telekinesis.' He told Fitz about the gun, and Sam's Italian trip. But Fitz was hardly listening. All he could think of was Maddie, her grip on his arm, the drops of silver rain in her hair, the hope on her face. The kiss on his cheek.

How was he going to tell her?

By the time they reached the Via Del Corso the sun had come out, and a fresh smell of soil and flowers filled the air. There was no trace of the demonstration: no broken placards, no smudges of soot, no fragments of glass. The street had been cleared up and hosed down. Even the gardens looked tidy. One broken window covered with loose paper, which flapped in the wind, was the only sign that anything had happened at all.

'It's lovely, isn't it?' Amazingly, Catelli made an attempt to take Sam's hand as they got out of the car. She tried not be too sudden about snatching it away, and tried to ignore the puzzled, hurt look he gave her. Was she being rude, by the standards of this time?

Catelli led along the wide pavement towards a corner café. 'This is where the policeman was robbed of his gun,' he said, sweeping his arms wide as if making a fresh, and rather melodramatic, TV commentary. Then he gave her a smile and a wink. She wondered whether he had anything to show her at all, or whether he was *only* trying to chat her up.

'And here…' he said, bending down.

Sam saw something scratched on the pavement – a crude circle with a capital R inside it. It was the symbol that the Revolution Man had carved on the pyramids.

'The international symbol of Revolution – of the new freedom,' commented Catelli. 'You've seen it before, of course.'

'Hmm.' Sam looked more closely. It wasn't scratched or carved: it was *gouged* out. It looked like a mark made by a giant finger, a child playing in clay. But the paving slab was big and solid. It should have cracked under that sort of pressure. She couldn't think of any twentieth-century human technology that could have done it.

She remembered the dancing gun, her discussion with the Doctor about telekinesis and invisibility, and wondered again who had been here.

'Not human, anyway,' she muttered. Who had invisibility technology? Who could cold-melt stone? Selachians? Zygons? The sun was hot on the back of her neck.

'Oh-oh,' said Catelli suddenly.

Sam could hear footsteps approaching. From long experience she recognised them as official – the heavy tread of policemen's boots.

Nonetheless she wasn't quite prepared for it when she stood up to see two smart men in blue uniforms pointing machine guns at her.

'Put your hands on your head,' said one. 'And don't move. You are under arrest.'

Sam put her hands on her head and sighed. Obviously someone had blown her cover, and she had a pretty good idea who that was.

It was going to be a long day.

Chapter Five

When Maddie got back to the house at Shooters Hill, Ed was sprawled on the tangerine couch in the sitting room, in his purple and gold dressing gown, with a copy of *Music Week* in his hands. Mick Jagger scowled from the front cover.

'Anything interesting?' asked Maddie.

'Yup,' said Ed. 'My lady's off in the park with another man.'

Maddie closed her eyes, felt a shiver of guilt and pain run through her. She knew she'd already lost the argument, even though it hadn't started.

Nonetheless, she tried. 'He's nice,' she said. 'And a perfect gentleman.'

'I wondered why there weren't any stains on the couch.'

Maddie crumpled into a chair, feeling physically sick. She wondered what had happened to 'fun', to 'laid back', to 'having a ball'.

'Do it outside, did you?'

'Ed, we didn't "do it" at all.'

Ed raised the paper across his face. 'Have it your way.'

Ed's bare feet were sticking out over the arm of the sofa, soles dirty, toes curling and uncurling.

'He won't seem so glamorous once you're up close to him.' Her mother had said that. Maddie had thought she was being naive and old-fashioned – but now she knew what the remark had meant.

No, she thought. It was all right until we took that damn drug. We had three months together and it was all right.

Then we killed three hundred and sixty-one people. And

I'm blaming him and he's trying to pretend it didn't matter.

With an effort, she walked across to Ed and put a hand on his shoulder.

'Sorry,' she said. 'I was trying to find out something.' Ed grunted. 'About Om-Tsor.'

He jolted under her hand, dropped the paper in his lap.

'You *told* him about Om-Tsor?'

'He's a psychic investigator.'

'Don't be stupid! I told you not to tell *anyone*. If *anyone* finds out –'

'We didn't necessarily do it.'

'*What?*'

Maddie told him about her theory of psychic resonance, adding, 'Fitz thinks it might be true. He wants a sample of Om-Tsor so that he can find out.'

Ed shook his head, spoke gently. 'There are things you don't know, baby. Things you don't want to know, believe me.' He put a hand over hers. 'Just trust me. It's better that you don't tell him any more.'

'But if he could find out how it worked –'

'No way, baby.' He stood up, hugged her, spoke into her ear. 'I know what you did was terrible, but it was a mistake, OK? An accident. You weren't responsible. Telling other people you did it can only make things worse for you. It'll be in the papers, on the news. You don't want that, do you?'

Maddie shook her head. She felt Ed's breath on her ear, then his lips against her cheek, the side of her neck.

'Bad publicity,' he murmured.

She giggled.

The prison smelled of a pungent smoke. Sam had seen it

rising from spiral burners in the passageways. Her cellmate said that it was to kill the mosquitoes. 'We can live in the stink of our own urine, but we mustn't get mosquito bites,' she said, gesturing at the bucket in the corner of their cell.

Her name was Pippa and she was English. Her hair was short and blonde, like Sam's, and her face was dirty and aggressive. Sam guessed she was about eighteen.

'Were you picked up at the demo?' she asked.

Pippa shrugged. 'Sorry, but I can't tell you. You're not in our group, and I can't tell anyone anything if they're not in our group.'

Sam nodded. 'In case I'm a spy.'

'Yeah. Sorry, nothing personal.'

'It's OK.'

There was a short silence. Sam glanced up at the narrow bar of light that was the only window, and decided that it was about five o'clock. How long could they detain her without trial? Not more than a day, surely. But this was a prison, not a police station. Outside, she could hear the clatter of doors and the shouting of warders as inmates were marched out, for exercise, or perhaps a meal.

'In China they don't put people in prison,' said Pippa. She stood up and peered through the narrow barred slot in the door. 'They re-educate them. The former Emperor has been re-educated as a gardener. He loves it.'

Sam decided to ignore this. It was hopeless arguing with someone who believed a propaganda story, and anyway Pippa's views on China weren't important. 'Have you been before the magistrate yet?' she asked.

'Sorry, can't answer that either.'

Sam felt a surge of annoyance. 'Oh, come on, Pippa. That's

hardly a state secret!'

The younger woman turned and glared at her, then shrugged. 'It's all about voluntary co-operation,' she said. 'If you create the right circumstances, people will work together without coercion, and without the need for any profit motive.'

'And in the wrong circumstances they won't work together. They won't even tell each other whether they've been before the magistrate. Or how long we can be held here without charge.'

Pippa turned to her and gave a brilliant smile. 'That's it exactly! In an oppressive condition such as this, everybody is everybody else's enemy. Once you break the oppressive condition, then everybody is everybody's friend.'

'And how do you break the oppressive condition?'

'Oh, you have to use violence.' Pippa smiled. 'That's why they arrested me.'

'I can see that,' said Sam, thinking, *I've been here before*. She wondered whether Pippa was one of Jean-Pierre's disciples. It seemed likely. Suddenly she wondered whether Rex's influence had done as much good as later historians had imagined. What was the use of an intelligent idea in the hands of a stupid person?

Pippa flung herself down on the bed. 'It's thirty-six hours, actually.'

'Before they have to charge you?'

'And then they need evidence.'

'What kind of evidence?'

Pippa didn't reply.

Sam paced up and down the narrow cell for a while, stood on tiptoe to gaze out of the window but saw only a blue sky.

Pippa sat up again. 'We ought to start a protest.'

'I don't see any easy way of communicating with anyone in a neighbouring cell,' said Sam. 'And besides, I don't think a protest would help in a situation like this.' But then I'm not a young, ill-informed anarchist with an almost insane idealism, not much intelligence, and no clear mission.

Pippa only snorted. Sam decided that the younger woman was probably just bored. It would be best to keep Pippa busy, while she thought up a more sensible plan. 'OK. What kind of protest?' she asked.

'We could set fire to the bunks.'

'That's, um, not very practical,' said Sam, trying not to laugh. 'We'd all choke on the fumes.'

Pippa did another of her shrugs. 'If the Revolution Man was here he'd just break down the walls.'

Sam laughed, to cover a feeling of gut astonishment. 'Who's the Revolution Man?' she asked. 'Oh, no, I forgot. You can't tell me that.'

'He's the spirit of anarchy. The spirit of freedom.' Pippa sounded as if she was reciting a mantra. 'He killed the policemen yesterday. It was them or us.'

Sam's feeling of excitement intensified. Pippa might just be angry and confused, but on the other hand –

'He's a real person then?' she asked. 'You've met him?'

Pippa went to the window and tried to look out, but she was shorter than Sam and couldn't quite make it.

'I've met him,' she said. 'Most of us have. You will, if you're for real.'

Again, Sam wondered whether Pippa was quite sane. The terms she was using sounded almost religious, as if she were a Christian describing the presence of Christ. Given the mysterious way the Revolution Man's signs appeared, this was understandable. But it wasn't much help.

Before she could ask any more questions Sam heard the sound of footsteps outside, followed by the turning of the key in the door. A warder appeared, the same hard-faced woman who had escorted Sam to her cell. With her was a small, rotund man in a grey suit.

'I'm your legal representative,' he said, without ceremony. 'You –' he pointed at Sam – 'are out on police bail, a Dr John Smith, English. Sign this, please. You –' to Pippa – 'are to appear before the judge tomorrow at ten o'clock.'

'Hey, wait a minute –' said Pippa.

Sam signed the papers, then murmured to the lawyer, 'Dr Smith will stand bail for Pippa too. He just didn't know she was in here.'

The lawyer nodded. 'Get in touch with him and I'll see. This is all ridiculous, you know.' He didn't say whether he meant the bail procedure or the fact that people had been arrested in the first place. Sam wondered whose side he was on.

'You're a stoolie, aren't you?' snapped Pippa from behind them.

Sam glanced over her shoulder. 'No. Just trying to get you out.'

'I don't believe you,' said Pippa stubbornly. Her face was dark with anger. Sam knew there was no hope of finding anything more about the Revolution Man now. Reluctantly, she let the little lawyer lead her away to freedom.

Not for the first time, the Doctor had mistimed a rescue.

Fitz looked at his watch again. It was nearly seven o'clock, and it was beginning to get dark. He looked up at the shadowed dome of the observatory, low grey clouds running above it, and decided he'd probably been stood up. He shuffled his shoes on the path and hugged his chest, and wished it was a bit warmer. The shoes were new. He'd bought them in Oxford Street, together with an up-to-the-minute brand-name shirt and blue jeans, all with the Doctor's money.

All for nothing. She wasn't coming, that much was obvious. And it had taken him an hour to convince himself. Pathetic.

He started back down the path that led to the front entrance and the river. He could catch a number 73 back across the river, and walk to Mile End tube station.

About halfway down he heard a shout.

'Hey! Fitz!'

Maddie.

His heart jumped rather more than he wanted it to. He wasn't really falling for her, was he? He'd thought he was old enough to know the difference between flirtation and the real thing.

Perhaps he wasn't. Perhaps no one ever was.

Maddie was running down the hill. For a moment he thought she was going to run into his arms, but she stopped just in time. She stood there, out of breath, her face pale in the darkening air. 'Hi,' she said.

'Well?' he asked, when she didn't say any more.

'I told him in the end.'

'Ed?' He felt faint, irritating grumbles of jealousy, as distracting and embarrassing as indigestion. 'What did he –'

'Oh, he was mad about it at first. Then he got better. But he doesn't want you to do anything. He says…' She shrugged, a little wildly. 'He says we just have to live with it.' She began to back away.

'You can't,' said Fitz.

'I have to go. He's doing a concert at half past seven. I've got to be there.'

Fitz started up the path after her. 'The Doctor – that's my boss – he says this needs looking into. You might not be the only people who've got hold of this stuff. It's a matter of saving lives – we need that sample, Maddie.'

She carried on walking, but said, 'I don't know.' Then she stopped, turned to him, and almost screamed out the words, 'I don't know, Fitz, I don't know. Is that all right? I think I've killed hundreds of people and I don't know what the truth is and I'm tired of thinking about it.'

They stood in the mild wind, staring at each other for a few moments.

'Do you know where he keeps it?' asked Fitz at last.

'The chimney breast in the attic,' said Maddie. 'But –'

Push the advantage. 'And he's out now?'

Maddie nodded. 'OK. But if he finds out –'

'He won't. We won't need a lot.' The Doctor hadn't said how much, presumably because he wasn't sure what they were dealing with. Fitz decided he would have to – what was that phrase Sam used? – 'wing it'.

They passed the observatory and crossed Blackheath. It was quiet, traffic rumbling along the road beyond a line of young trees. The light had faded, gained that almost glasslike quality of dusk. A squirrel bolted across the grass: grey. He remembered that there had been red squirrels, once. The Doctor had said you couldn't change things like that. 'Too many threads, Fitz,' he'd said. 'Too many little changes.'

If it was all fixed, why worry? Why was he doing this, here, now? Who was he trying to save? People would die, or they wouldn't. Maddie would probably marry Ed. He would go off in the TARDIS and do something else where the results were preordained.

Or were they? He would have to ask the Doctor about it some time. But would the Doctor tell the truth? Did he know?

They reached the house. 'It seems an odd choice, for a rock star,' Fitz commented to Maddie, gesturing at the thirties suburbia around them. He hadn't thought about it last night: too drunk, too interested in Maddie.

'He's got a flat in West Ken,' she said. 'For parties and things. He'll drop round there after the gig. This is his hideaway. His investment, he says.'

'That's sensible,' commented Fitz. But it seemed too sensible, too modest somehow. Or was he just looking for clues where there weren't any?

Maddie went into the house first, just to make sure that none of Ed's friends were there. A light flicked on upstairs, and Maddie leaned out of a window. 'All clear!'

Fitz went in, up the stairs, feeling as if he were about to embark on an illicit love affair. Perhaps he was. Maddie met him on the landing. The skin of her face was slightly flushed, as if she too was thinking –

'Up here.' A flight of wooden steps, a hole in the roof.

The attic at least was hardly suburban. Fitz took in the fake stained-glass window, the goat's skull, the Buddha. It looked horribly pretentious, the kind of false eclecticism that people like –

People like Fitz himself indulged in, for instance. It took a taste of the Doctor's genuine, millennia-old, alien time-travelling eclecticism to make you realise how little point there was in being pretentious.

Maddie was fiddling with the chimney breast, which was painted with strange, crude flowers against a deep-green background. Fitz found the mural slightly disturbing. She emerged with a dark box, which she opened slowly.

Then she took a breath. 'It's gone!'

Fitz peered inside, saw the dark wood, a couple of white flakes that looked like butterfly wings. He touched one of them. 'Is this it?'

'Yes, but the box was full. He must have moved it.' She began rummaging around in the attic, moving from place to place quickly, clumsily.

Fitz picked up the white flake, felt only a papery dryness. He sniffed it, but it had no smell.

'I'll take what there is,' he said, hoping this would be enough for the Doctor.

'Shh!' Maddie was standing above the trapdoor, looking down at the landing. 'There's someone coming!'

Fitz frowned. Quickly, he slipped the two flakes of Om-Tsor into the sample packet the Doctor had provided, then pushed the box back into its hideaway. He couldn't immediately see the loose brick that Maddie must have removed.

Below, he heard the front door open.

'I'll go down,' whispered Maddie.

Fitz heard her descending the wooden stairs. 'Ed, I can't find –'

Then silence, followed by a gunshot and a heavy thud.

Just for a second, Fitz froze. Then he shifted his weight, without moving his feet on the noisy attic floor, so that he could see a little through the trapdoor. He heard painful breathing – Maddie? – and footsteps. They were ascending the wooden stairs towards the attic. Fitz moved, very quickly, and got to the trapdoor just as the head and shoulders of a man came through. Fitz had time to register a slightly sallow skin, heavy brows – Chinese? Indian? – then he saw that there was a hand, too, a hand carrying a gun.

The gun was pointed at his chest, and he was dropping, dropping as the gun fired and –

Had he been hit? He wasn't sure.

A second shot, and Fitz kicked out at the man's gun hand. It dodged, but the gun jumped loose, fell down towards the landing. The man made an almost comical shrug, then clattered down the stairs after it. Fitz started after him, but he couldn't move as quickly. He reached the top of the main stairs just as the front door slammed, shaking the house.

The man was gone. The gun was gone. But at the bottom of the stairs Maddie was sprawled on her face. Fitz could see blood soaking the back of her coat, could hear her ragged breathing. He stopped three steps up, swaying, almost gagging with shock. He knelt down, put a finger on Maddie's neck, felt a weak pulse. Her eyes were closed, but she was whispering something.

He leaned close to her, heard the words, 'I should have gone home' repeated over and over, like a mantra.

Chapter Six

Signor Catelli was waiting outside the prison, eating a green ice-cream cone. Sam remembered that the variety was called pistachio.

'I didn't think you would be in long,' he said, with an elaborate wink. 'Ice cream?' He gestured at the cone, at a nearby café with white tables on the pavement and scruffily dressed young people arguing and drinking coffee.

Sam shook her head.

'A walk, then?'

Sam frowned at him. She wasn't sure she liked his company and, anyway, he'd told her all he could. Or had he? Nonetheless she followed him a street between tall ochre buildings with shutters closing for the night and low lamps sending slatted light out over balconies. The pavement was crowded, most of the people moving in the opposite direction to Sam and Catelli. It made staying together difficult and conversation even more so.

'So,' he said. 'What sort of report will you be making to your superiors?'

'Well, I'm sorry, signor, but I won't be mentioning the spirit of the revolution.'

He grabbed her arm, the same one that Rex had wrenched. This grip, too, was almost painful.

'Neither will I,' he said. 'Come on. It's the truth I need.'

She glanced at him sidelong. Suddenly it clicked: he was some kind of intelligence agent. Which implied that he thought she was one, too. She remembered his close inspection of her letter of introduction.

Damn the Doctor. He never quite thought these details through.

Catelli was still holding her arm hard, piloting her through the crowd. It occurred to her that she might be piloted to a nearby car, spirited away. She's seen it happen in Cold War movies. Had it happened in real life? She wondered which power bloc Catelli was working for, and who he thought she was.

Carefully she said, 'You know, I found very little. Some graffiti.'

Catelli nodded. 'Exactly my conclusions. Yet the weapon is real. I wonder who – the third party, perhaps? Do you think it possible?'

Sam nodded, though she had no idea who or what he was talking about. 'It's possible,' she said. 'We'll look into it.'

'I dare say we all will.' He released her arm, almost pushed her into a market stall. The owner was packing up, putting loose fruit into boxes.

When Sam looked around Catelli was gone into the crowds and the dusk.

The ambulance seemed to be taking forever to arrive. Maddie had stopped talking, though her face twitched from time to time. Fitz had risked moving her into the recovery position, despite the injury. He hoped he'd got it right. Sam's first-aid training suddenly seemed terribly limited. What happened if Maddie stopped breathing?

He looked at her again and saw that she was shivering violently.

Shock, he thought. She's in shock. I should have covered

her straight away. He ran up the stairs, plunged into a room, saw a bed and ripped the counterpane and blankets from it. He almost fell down the stairs carrying the clumsy burden.

When he reached Maddie the skin of her face was grey and she was shaking violently. He threw the blanket over her, but she kept shaking.

She's going to die, he thought. Where *is* the ambulance? He strained his ears but heard no bells. Weren't they supposed to respond within two minutes?

Then he realised what he had to do. What he should have done in the first place. He went back to the phone, found a telephone directory, and scrabbled through the flimsy pages until he found the Alhambra Hotel.

The phone rang for a long time, until Fitz began to worry if there would be an answer. The rings seemed to time themselves with Maddie's breathing. He wondered if he should go and comfort her. At last the phone was answered. Fitz didn't wait for the woman to finish speaking, just gabbled out his request to speak to the Doctor.

'We don't take private calls.'

'It's an emergency. Someone's dying.'

Maddie gave a little gasp, and her breathing became even more unsteady. Belatedly it occurred to Fitz that she might still be conscious.

'Fitz?' The Doctor's voice. Fitz felt a surge of relief.

'We need the TARDIS here. Shooters Hill. Now.' He gave the full address. 'Maddie's been shot.'

'I'll be there as quickly –'

'Not "as quickly", Doctor. *Now*. Get to the TARDIS, and bring it back in time to here, now.'

A slight pause. 'Fitz, it's dangerous to have the TARDIS in

two places at the same time, so close to each other. It could affect the whole of space-time. Besides, I'm not sure if –'

'If you don't do it, she'll die.'

Another pause. 'I'll do what I can. Wait there.' Fitz heard him speaking at a distance from the mouthpiece. 'You don't happen to have a motorbike I can borrow?' Then the line went dead.

Fitz went to Maddie. For a moment he thought her breathing had stopped, then she made a single deep, whooping breath.

He had a feeling that it wasn't a very good sign.

From outside, he heard the roar of an engine, and the clatter of bells. 'The ambulance is here,' he told Maddie. 'Everything will be all right now.'

She gave another whooping breath, and her eyelids twitched.

There was a knock at the door. Fitz opened it. The ambulanceman was young, probably younger than Fitz. When he saw Maddie, his face went pale.

'She's been shot!' He crouched down over her.

'Yes,' said Fitz.

'Have you informed the police?' His fingers were on her neck, searching for a pulse.

'I've been trying to save her life.'

A second man pushed past Fitz, exchanged a glance with his comrade, who slowly shook his head. Fitz felt a hand on his shoulder. 'I'm sorry, sir, you'd better come outside a minute.'

No, thought Fitz. And: This is my fault. She wouldn't have been here if I hadn't insisted on getting that sample.

Outside, the wind seemed colder than before. Fitz

shivered. The ambulance was painted silver, curiously bright under the street lamps. The back doors were open.

The man led Fitz to the wall at the end of the garden. 'Sit down a minute.'

Fitz sat.

'Cigarette?'

Fitz nodded, lit up, puffed desperately. Nothing happened, no soothing, no feeling better, only a burning in his throat. He coughed.

'Are you her husband?' asked the man.

Fitz shrugged. 'Just a friend. I don't even live here.'

'Who are her next of kin?'

'I don't know. Her… the man who lives here, they were… engaged, I think. He's a musician, he's playing tonight.'

'And her family?'

'I don't know.'

A pause. 'She's dead.'

'I know.'

'The police will be here soon. We'll stay until they arrive.'

Fitz nodded again. He knew they suspected him of killing Maddie.

'Someone broke in,' he said, trying to put some certainty and authority into his voice. 'They had a gun. I've no idea what they were after. I don't think they were expecting anyone to be in. He shot Maddie. He tried to shoot me –'

'You'd better tell that to the police.'

Inside the ambulance, a radio crackled. The man got up, walked across, lifted the bulky microphone, and spoke briefly. Then listened.

He ran inside, then emerged with his colleague.

'We're going to have to go!' he shouted at Fitz. 'There's a big fire at Wembley. Stay here and wait for the police, right?'

Fitz nodded, stood up, stubbed the cigarette out on the wall. The ambulance started up and roared away down the road.

Fitz waited.

He was expecting it, but the whisper, the blue shimmer, then the whooping roar of the materialising TARDIS still shocked him, still made the hairs on his neck prickle. The final thud as the blue police box solidified shook the windows of the house.

The door opened, and the Doctor got out, carrying a leather briefcase in one hand and a motorcycle crash helmet in the other.

'You're too late!' snarled Fitz.

But the Doctor shook his head. 'Not necessarily!' He was already running down the path. Fitz followed, wondering if the Doctor thought he could bring back the dead.

And if he could bring back the dead...

What would that make him?

The whipped chocolate froth of the cappuccino was sweet, but it made the coffee hard to drink. Sam was sure she was acquiring a moustache of foam as she determinedly sipped away. Around her, the café was beginning to get noisy. Women in short, bright dresses, men in equally bright shirts. Sam saw the glint of jewelled rings and chokers, and decided that this was probably not a cheap café. She hadn't checked how much her drink would be: everything was in thousands of lira anyway, and she hadn't bothered to convert it. Good job she was on expenses.

She grinned at the thought: TARDIS expenses. The

Doctor's infinite-seeming bank accounts, investments, platinum credit cards. Perhaps he secretly held the whole world's economy together, subtly directed it, kept it going. She wouldn't put it past him.

She noticed that a man was looking at her. He was dressed in a smart but rather dull suit, and sitting with two similarly attired companions. They didn't look as if they were on holiday, somehow. Their body language was that of civil servants. And the one who was watching her was… well, watching. He didn't look flirtatious. He didn't even look friendly.

Well, there were three choices. She could wait, she could walk away, she could walk up to them.

She took a deep breath, then stood up, cappuccino in her hand, and weaved her way between the glittering café-goers.

'Hi,' she said to the men in suits. 'I'm Sam Jones. Who are you?'

The man glanced at his companions. 'This isn't a game, miss,' he said seriously. 'We know you were with Catelli. We'd like to know what you said to him.'

Sam shrugged. There was no reason not to tell the truth. 'I asked him about the flying gun incident that was on the news. He said it was "the spirit of the revolution" and showed me something carved in the pavement.'

'You met him today. After he got you released from prison.'

'He didn't. My boss did that.'

They didn't ask who her boss was, which was interesting. Instead the three men stood up.

'If you'd like to come with us…'

'Why should I?' asked Sam, but they didn't answer. Two of the men were behind her, not quite touching her, but close.

Other customers in the café were glancing up, puzzled. Sam knew that if she ran, *now*, she would probably get away. But she wasn't sure she wanted to. Whatever variety of officialdom these people were, they probably knew more than she did. So she let them hustle her towards a long black Jaguar parked half on the pavement, let them push her gently into the back seat.

'Now, then, miss,' said the spokesman, sitting down next to her. 'I want you to tell the truth. Who you work for. Who built the weapon. Who they're selling it to.'

Sam began to laugh. 'Well, I don't know any of those things.'

The man seemed nonplussed for a moment, then he laughed too, but in a forced way. 'We still need to know what you were doing with Catelli,' he insisted.

Sam laughed again. 'Well, we didn't talk in lines of dialogue from old films,' she said.

This time he didn't even attempt to laugh in return. Sam decided her interrogator didn't have much imagination. His face was square, pasty – he looked as if hadn't seen the sun for a while.

The car was pulling away, cruising down the street, tyres rumbling gently on the road. Sam remembered that she hadn't paid for her cappuccino.

'Perhaps you'd better tell me who you are,' she told her interrogator.

He told her.

And then she told the truth.

He didn't believe her, of course.

'Not a miracle,' the Doctor said, when Maddie started breathing again. 'Not a miracle at all.'

The TARDIS medical room was quiet, organic. Fitz stared at the ghostly blue tracery of the surgical web, at the winking lights of the lasers cutting away damaged flesh, the glittering robots that the Doctor called 'healers' patching in pieces of organic polymer, as tiny and translucent as butterfly wings.

'I've seen miracles,' the Doctor went on, 'and this isn't one. If this had been nineteen ninety-seven instead of nineteen sixty-seven even human paramedics could have saved her.' He went on to explain about brain death and parameters and oxygen-starvation levels, but it was still a miracle to Fitz. All he could do was watch the slow return of life to Maddie's cheeks, the slow rise and fall of her chest.

She was *alive*.

After about twenty minutes the Doctor announced with some satisfaction that Maddie was stabilised.

It was only then that Fitz remembered the other 'butterfly wings', the drug that it had all been about. He got out the sample packet and showed it to the Doctor. The Doctor did exactly what Fitz himself had done: he felt the white flakes, smelled them. Then he nodded.

'Rubasdpofiaew,' he said. 'Sorry, but that's the nearest to the correct sound I can make. It's a powerful telekinetic, used by the nonsentient brasdpods of Tau Ceti Minor to help them catch their food. From memory it's a sort of plant – these look quite fresh.' He frowned. 'If it's growing on Earth it could be serious. Sentient beings usually can't use it – but if it works for humans...' He glanced at Maddie. 'We need to find the source of this, and we need to find it soon. There are people out there who want to change the world, and they're willing to try anything. They won't understand this – they'll think it's a game, a mind-blowing experience like the other stuff that's around. By the time they find out it's real it could be too late. And then there are other people –' He broke off. 'Anything's possible. The danger is grave, believe me.'

Fitz looked at Maddie, swaddled in the strange flowing colours of the TARDIS's surgical equipment. 'It already is,' he pointed out.

'It could be a lot worse than one train crash.' The Doctor looked down. 'When Maddie comes round there are some questions I need to ask her. I want you to go and see if you can find… Ed? Was it Ed?' Fitz nodded. 'Find him, and bring him here. It doesn't matter what pretext you use.'

'I'll just say –' He gestured at Maddie.

'Yes, yes, yes. Go on!'

Fitz found himself being hustled out of the door of the surgery and into the console room. He blinked, confused. He was sure that he hadn't come in this way, and that the console room didn't normally have a door to anything that might be called a surgery – but here he was, standing on the old carpet, beside the clocks. The car that the Doctor kept in the console room was partly dismembered at the moment, oily components spread on a stained cloth. A motorbike was parked next to the car.

The TARDIS main doors were open: outside, he saw a police car, parked against the kerb. There was no one inside it. He stepped out, moved around the TARDIS and walked away. He expected a shout from behind, the shrill of a police whistle, but nothing happened.

At the top of the hill, he looked back, and saw just a sleepy street, a few lights in the houses, a police car, a police box. Hard to believe that someone had almost died, that the police box was a vast space-time ship, that an alien drug was endangering the world. He tried to think about how much damage Om-Tsor could do, but he could think only about Maddie, gasping for breath, dying because someone had thought it easier to kill her than to worry about the consequences of keeping her alive.

Then he realised what the Doctor had meant by 'other people'. People like Ed and Maddie might do some damage by accident, maybe even serious damage. But whoever had been trying to get hold of Om-Tsor tonight was more deadly than that. What would happen if Om-Tsor got into their hands? It was potentially as bad as the bomb – perhaps worse.

Which meant that a lot of people were probably after it.

Fitz glanced about him nervously as he reached the main road, then flagged down a taxi.

'Thurcott's,' he said, hoping he'd remembered the name of the venue correctly. 'Quickly.'

Rome Centre, as Alan called it, was a small sitting room in the back of an ornate villa belonging to the British Embassy. Silk-striped chairs and a silk-striped sofa filled the space between walls stuccoed in sienna. A marble bust of Disraeli stood guard at the door. Alan was her chief interrogator, the smallest of the three men who'd picked her up from the café. In this setting, in his formal grey suit, he looked like a bank manager.

Sam decided she'd probably find him quite scary as a bank manager, but as an interrogator he was about as terrifying as the sleepy bloodhound he in some ways resembled. But she knew better than to be fooled by appearances. These people might not be as bad as the KGB, but if they decided she was working for the KGB – or anyone else that they didn't like – things might get rough.

At the moment, they were being polite.

'So,' said Alan, with an air of weary patience, as if she'd taken out an unauthorised overdraft. 'You're working for an organisation that doesn't exist until next year. What are we supposed to do, miss? Hold you in Holloway until then, and see if this Lethbridge-Stewart backs you up?'

'Wouldn't it be easier to tell the truth?' This from one of the other men. They hadn't introduced themselves, just hung around, overfilling the silk-striped armchairs and trying to look large and threatening.

'I am telling the truth,' said Sam simply. 'I'm not working for any foreign power, and I had no idea who Catelli was until he as good as told me –'

'Yes, well, Catelli never did have any sense,' said Alan with a smile.

'So why don't you –'

Glass shattered, and everyone looked up. The floor was shaking.

Alan looked at Sam. 'What the –'

Sam shrugged.

A crack was spidering across the ceiling, and the floor was shaking enough to send the marble bust of Disraeli teetering.

Alan's minders were standing up, staring around in bewilderment. An alarm went off, a continuous bell. Somewhere, more windows shattered.

'Outside!' yelled Sam.

Alan stared at her.

'If it's an earthquake we're safer –'

A loud bang. Disraeli had fallen off his perch.

Sam decided she wasn't going to wait around and see what else fell over. She ran to the door. It was locked. Alan pushed her aside, quite roughly, and fumbled with a bunch of keys attached to his waist.

The building stopped shaking. There was a last distant thud, then silence.

Alan opened the door. 'You're still our guest,' he observed. His voice was shaking.

Sam merely nodded.

They all ran through the long, tiled corridor that led to the front door. The tiles were cracked, and covered in chunks of fallen plaster.

The front door wasn't there at all.

Outside, a confused crowd milled in the street. The traffic was stopped. A woman was curled up on the pavement, sobbing. Most other people were staring at the building.

Sam stumbled down the steps, almost tripping over pieces of stone. 'Mind the glass!' shouted somebody.

She found a clear stretch of pavement, turned and looked up.

The front of the building had a hole in it. At first Sam couldn't discern the shape, but then, because she was looking for it, because she'd expected it, she saw the circle, the capital R carved out in the middle. Broken bricks, torn-off floorboards, fragments of glass, all distorted the icon, but it was there.

A dead body was slumped across one of the walls. It was a young woman, her rumpled dress stained with blood.

Feeling a little sick, Sam turned, saw Alan talking to an Italian policeman. She strode up to him, tapped him on the shoulder.

'You've got to believe me now,' she said. 'And you've got to believe me quickly. Because we're probably going to need your help.'

He looked at her, his eyes suddenly cold, judging, not like a bloodhound or a bank manager at all.

Then he nodded. 'Maybe,' he said. 'We'll see.'

Chapter Seven

'You can't come in now, mate.'

The doorman was half as tall again as Fitz, and probably six times as heavy. Behind him, the hall hummed with music, a heavy, sensual thudding beat shaking the floor. Fitz could hear women in the audience screaming, the way they had for the Beatles before he'd left in 1963. Perhaps they did it for everyone now.

Fitz looked up at the doorman, met cold blue eyes and a shiny hairless dome. The man could almost have been a Sontaran from one of the Doctor's holiday pics, if he'd been a bit darker.

'I've got a message about Ed's girlfriend. She's seriously hurt.'

'I'll pass it on.'

Somehow Fitz doubted this. 'I'm his friend,' he insisted.

The doorman gave Fitz a measuring look. 'Aren't we all, mate?' he said. He glanced over his shoulder. 'Bloke here wants to talk to Ed. Says his girlfriend's hurt.'

Laughter. 'That's a good one. Sure it isn't his pet rabbit got a sore foot?'

'She may not have long to live.' Fitz felt a faint lurch in his stomach, at the thought that this might still be true. He remembered Maddie's grey face, her last, gasping breaths. The Doctor had said she would be all right now. He was telling the truth, wasn't he?

The doorman frowned. 'Charlie, get Frank. I think we might have a problem here.'

Charlie laughed. 'I still reckon it's the pet rabbit.'

'Go and get Frank!'

Fitz waited. The wind blowing down the street was cold. There wasn't much traffic. From inside the building, the beat still rumbled, slowing, stuttering, like a faltering heart. Then it stopped.

'What happened to her?' asked the doorman.

Fitz hesitated. 'She was shot.'

The doorman swore, shook his head, then stepped aside. 'Go on in. Tell 'em Ray says it's OK.'

Inside, it was hot. The heat of spotlights, body heat. The heat permeated the passageways that led to the stage door, wafted from doorways. A young woman was sprawled in one of the passageways, her head in the lap of a young man.

'It's cool,' said the man, looking up. His hair was long, greasy. 'She fainted. It's OK.'

Fitz just stepped past them. He could taste smoke in the air. The thunder of music had started again, and Fitz could hear a regular chant, mesmeric, even a little frightening.

He saw two men in suits ahead, talking, their bodies half lit by sidelong light from an open door.

'Ray says it's OK,' said Fitz. He had to shout, over the noise.

To his surprise, the man rushed forward and extended a hand. He had a small, sly face, and bright eyes.

'I'm Frank,' he said. 'We've just had a call from the police about –' His eyes slid towards the stage. 'I'll get him off. If you think it's best for you to… You're his friend?'

Fitz nodded.

The man disappeared into the light and noise. Fitz started to follow, was restrained by the other man's hand on his shoulder. Ahead, the stage was a glare of electric-blue smoke.

The guitars shone. The drum kit was a metallic mountain island, the singers iconic statues, long-faced. Fitz realised they were wearing masks. He wasn't sure which one was Ed.

The music was building up, the drum kit twitching. Frank looked strange, a swimmer in an alien sea, approaching one of the singers. Before he could get there, the man rose into the air. It was so swift, so sudden, that it seemed as if he'd jumped, but jumped impossibly far and high. He was soaring over the audience. The guitar fell, flashing like a meteor. Someone screamed.

Ed – it must be Ed – whirled around the domed roof several times, almost brushing the walls. The music had fallen silent in a patter of confused drumbeats, and all Fitz could hear was the scream.

Ed's scream. This wasn't supposed to happen. The audience weren't sure yet, suspecting wires, pulleys. But then there was a sound like an explosion, and there was a hole in the roof.

Two holes – three. More than three.

The drum kit whirled across stage in a jagged clatter of metal. The domed roof was lifting away, torn from the rest of the building. Fitz thought he saw Ed, hovering like a mosquito in the chaos of falling masonry.

Then there was only an empty sky, the clatter of loose bricks, Frank staggering back across the stage through scattering wisps of smoke. His suit was, strangely, unmarked, but there was blood running down his forehead.

The crowd started to scream again, this time in panic. Fitz saw a wave of motion towards the exits.

He ran out on to the stage, grabbed a microphone, praying it would still work.

'Stay where you are!' he barked, in his best military voice. 'There is no need for any panic. The worst is over. Please make your way to the exit nearest to you in an orderly way.' If they didn't they were going to get crushed.

At first people didn't seem to be taking much notice, but there was a gradual slowing of the movement when he repeated the instructions. Someone shouted, 'She's dead! She's dead!'

He heard another shout of 'I'm a doctor!'

Charlie was out on stage now too. He clapped Fitz on the shoulder. 'Frank's getting the cops in.' Into the microphone he added: 'OK, everyone, there's no need for panic.'

As he finished speaking, something fell from the now open roof and clattered down in the middle of the aisle. It bounced once, rolled in front of the stage.

It was Ed's long-faced mask, its gaudy colours stained with blood.

Sam knew she was being followed as soon as she left Heathrow Airport. They'd have been stupid to let her go without tailing her. He wasn't even taking the trouble to be all that discreet: the glances in her direction in the railway carriage, the footsteps only three or four metres behind her when she changed to a tube train. The same raincoat-clad figure in the next compartment on the underground train.

Sam wondered who the second, less obvious, follower was. There had to be one, surely. Or were the British security services as amateurish and incompetent as they seemed?

She wasn't all that surprised when the TARDIS wasn't in its place outside Earl's Court station. The pavement was empty. She looked around for Fallback One, the yellow sticky on a lamppost, failed to find it. But it had been raining: puddles decorated the pavement, and big clouds were still rambling across the sky.

OK, then. Fallback Two. She found a call box, dialled a Kent number. A rich, fruity voice answered, very English. 'Message box, please,' she said. 'S for Sam.'

A pause, a rustling of what sounded like sweet paper. 'The Alhambra Hotel,' said the voice after a while. 'Good luck!'

Sam grinned and hung up.

An hour later, when the wall-eyed clerk at the Alhambra said he'd gone missing on a motorbike the previous night, she was less amused. What could possibly have been so urgent that he hadn't left a message?

She tried the Kent number again, but there was no answer.

Damn.

Her tail was still with her, indiscreetly reading a newspaper, propped up against a wall. She went up to him. 'Hello.'

He lowered his newspaper and frowned at her. He was quite young, long-faced, his eyes pale blue and slightly protuberant.

'This isn't playing the game, is it?' she said, grinning. 'Look, I need to find someone. Quickly. Your lot can help.'

He stared at her blankly.

'Oh, come on. "Alan", whoever he is. We agreed to work together –'

'Your phone's ringing,' he observed.

Sam became aware of the repeater bell in the background, realised it came from the phone box. She ran across the road, narrowly avoiding a taxi, and answered it.

'Ah, Sam, I knew I'd find you here.' The Doctor's voice. 'You need to come to –' he gave an address in Shooters Hill – 'right now. I don't want to move the TARDIS again until I have to.'

'Doctor, there are things –'

'I know, I know, I *know*. You need to get here quickly!'

Sam wasn't sure whether the Doctor did know, but decided that there wasn't time to argue. 'All right. On my way.'

She had to hail a cab. She invited her tail to share it, which he did, somewhat ruefully.

'Not much point in this now, I suppose,' he said. 'But I have to make my report.'

Sam shrugged. There was no point in telling him that it didn't matter: once she was in the TARDIS he wouldn't be able to follow her anyway.

Nobody would.

Sometimes she wondered about that.

She looked out of the window at London passing her by, not speaking.

There was a sense of change, of small disarray, in the vast space of the console room. The doors weren't quite right, the feel of the light was different. Fitz was sitting in the Doctor's favourite chair, his chin in his hands, watching the clocks.

There was no sign of the Doctor. Sam raised an eyebrow at Fitz. 'How did you get on with the waitress?'

'Her name's Maddie.' He shrugged. 'She was shot and nearly died. Her boyfriend's been kidnapped by aliens. How did you get on?'

The summary almost made Sam smile, but Fitz's bleak expression killed the gesture. She too shrugged. 'I was arrested and imprisoned. When I got out I was questioned by the security services. The embassy in Rome was attacked by our friends –' She broke off. 'Are they aliens?'

'The Doctor's not sure. The drug is. It might be humans using it.' He stood up. 'The Doctor wants to take the TARDIS into the vortex, to track usage of Om-Tsor. But Maddie's still here.' He gestured vaguely behind him. 'Through there.'

'Does she want to leave?'

'She ought to go to a hospital.'

'She'd be better off here.' It was the Doctor's voice. Sam looked around, saw him bustling in from the library, a pile of books under his arm. 'But she's woken up, and she says she wants to go.'

Fitz stood up. 'I'll go with her.'

'We may not be back for a while,' said the Doctor.

'I know. But this is close to my own time. I quite like it.'

It was a moment before Sam realised what he meant. 'You mean you'd rather –'

Fitz looked at her, looked at the Doctor. 'I'm not sure. I like Maddie. We might be able to…' He shrugged. 'And even if not –'

'Yes, yes, yes, I understand,' said the Doctor briskly. 'You're quite sure, now?'

Fitz nodded.

Sam couldn't quite believe what was happening. She'd thought that Fitz might leave – but like this?

'Fitz, I'm not sure –' she began.

She couldn't believe he could want to go. She thought of what he'd been through when they'd first met, his mother going mad, dying, scaring the hell out of him, the police on his back. Had he just tried to escape all that, blundered on board because there was nowhere else to go? Second thoughts, now? Or maybe it was just that there'd be no one chasing him now, the heat well and truly off four years later. Or maybe he was bored already.

Christ, was it because she'd turned him down a couple of times now? Had he gone with the Doctor only because he fancied her? The idea was ridiculous. Wasn't it? But now he was leaving, apparently for no better reason than that he fancied someone else.

Fitz stuck out a hand. 'It's been good travelling with you, Sam. Keep in touch, if you can!' He gave a wink and a mock salute, which prevented Sam from shaking hands with him.

Just like Fitz.

She heard the sound of wheels behind her, saw the Doctor rolling a stretcher out of a door next to the library. A pale face, a wave of ginger hair. Wide eyes stared at the console room.

Sam helped Fitz wheel the stretcher outside. She wondered how they were going to get the young woman to a hospital. Then she saw a grey passageway, felt warm, stuffy air with a faint but distinct smell of antiseptic, and smiled. Trust the Doctor to sort things out smoothly. There was even a tag on Maddie's stretcher, presumably explaining her condition in medicalese.

She took all this in as they rolled the stretcher away from the TARDIS, which appeared to be inside a linen cupboard. She glanced up at Fitz. She wanted to say, 'Are you sure?', as the Doctor had, but his attention was all on Maddie's face.

She touched his shoulder. 'Good luck, Fitz.'

He glanced round, smiled. A nurse appeared from a doorway, looked down at the stretcher, clearly puzzled. 'Who…?'

Fitz began some explanations.

Sam backed gently away, towards the magic box in the linen cupboard that could travel through forever.

The Lion, the Witch and the Wardrobe, she thought. Here we go again.

Inside, the Doctor was attacking the console with both hands, his cuffs rolled up. Indicators flashed, the time rotor flooded with light.

He gave Sam a brilliant smile.

'Come on, Sam! There's work to do!'

Press Reports 1967–8

The Times, 28 December 1967:

Following the bizarre reports last month of a strange circular symbol appearing overnight on the face of the Great Pyramid, tourists returning from the ski resort of St Anton in Austria report seeing the same symbol sketched in the snow above the resort. The design, a circle with a capital R inside it, is said to be over 200 feet across.

Scientists are still puzzled by the 'freak weathering' of the pyramid, which occurred on the night of 5th November. The Egyptian government is taking seriously claims that an Israeli secret weapon may be involved. However, both Israel and the US State Department have denied that any such weapon is involved.

Since November the symbol has appeared on several public buildings and monuments throughout the world, including the Lincoln Memorial in Washington, one of the stones of Stonehenge, and the white cliffs of Dover. Whilst scientists remain baffled by the carvings, mystics claim that they are signs that a 'world revolution' will soon occur.

This latest appearance of the symbol seems to support the theory that some mysterious force is involved, since the area is surely too large to have been carved out by hand. Whether this force is a mystical sign, or simply a weapon gone wrong, remains to be seen.

San Francisco Chronicle, 14 February 1968:

The 'Big R', the symbol of the mysterious 'Revolution Man',

has appeared on both towers of the Golden Gate bridge in San Francisco.

Some young San Franciscans are claiming that the signs are messages from the 'Revolution Man', a messianic figure who they claim will fulfill their dream of uniting the world under a banner of love and peace.

However, Lt Marco Phillips of the San Francisco Police Department says: 'This is just another in a series of acts of vandalism designed to promote the activities of drug-takers and draft-dodgers. I have no time for these people. They have done thousands of dollars worth of damage to City property and they will be arrested.'

La Stampa, 15 March 1968 (trans.):

The appearance of the symbol of the Revolution Man on the floor of St Peter's Cathedral has brought about amazement and consternation in the Vatican. Pope Paul VI is known to be deeply concerned, and it is believed that he considers this the most serious of crimes.

It must be emphasised, however, that rumours that His Holiness has called a secret Council of Exorcists into being, for the first time since the 14th century, are just that: rumours. 'There is no supernatural element to this,' says a spokesman for His Holiness. 'It is merely the work of foolish young people who wish to undermine the teachings of Christ and go their own way in the world.'

Pravda, 29 April 1968 (trans.):

The despoliation of Red Square by lackeys of Western

imperialism shows the decadence of the capitalist system at its worst.

Thousands of loyal Soviet citizens have joined hands on the streets in a spontaneous outburst of indignation and protest at this heinous crime against the peace-loving government of the Soviet Union. The Moscow Cement Workers Co-operative No. 284 (West) has donated 300 tonnes of cement to repair the damage caused by the imperialist weapon.

In a speech last night, the General Secretary of the Soviet Communist Party Central Committee, Comrade Leonid Brezhnev, condemned the unprovoked imperialist attack on the Soviet people, and stated that any further aggression would be met with equivalent action. Comrade Brezhnev further said: 'The forces of imperialist and capitalist aggression cannot be allowed to escape the consequences of their provocative action against the heroic Soviet people.'

Book Two
1968

Chapter Eight

The sky was blue, a pure June blue. Sam took a deep breath of the air: it smelled of grass and flowers, but also of dust and sweat and cow dung. There was already a crowd: a buzzing, irregular crowd, talking, smoking, dressed in bright motley, moving from place to place, looking for some action. There was music, a dull booming that didn't resolve itself. The sound wasn't quite like thunder: distant mortar fire, perhaps, with random guitar accompaniment.

Some people had arrived on motorcycles, and these were parked on the track by the barn, their paint and chrome dulled by brown dust. Most, however, had walked, and were still walking, crowding the narrow road from Alton to East Worldham, bunching at the gate, scrambling through and running across the field in pink and blue and brown jackets, in old trousers, in bright shirts stencilled with flowers. And, yes, there was a girl with flowers in her hair, a ragtag of cow parsley and poppies picked from the ditches along the road.

The Doctor was smiling. He was running up and down the gentle slope between barn and gate like an excitable puppy, greeting people. He seemed to blend in, despite his incongruous costume, or perhaps because of it. If ever there was a natural member of the hippie generation, it was him. The people he greeted probably assumed he was one of the festival organisers, a flower child like themselves, but Sam knew that half an hour ago he'd been deadly serious, his face dark, his eyes on the new space-time anomaly that the TARDIS had detected during the festival. Now all that seemed to be forgotten, though Sam knew better. He was searching, without seeming to search.

Sam was supposed to be talking to people, too. But she was finding it harder going. She could feel the mood of youth and innocence, as thick as honey, as sentimental as an old Technicolor movie – but she couldn't quite join in. This was a revolution, yeah. It had changed the world, yeah. But Sam could only see a field full of rather aimless people who didn't quite know what they were protesting against or what they were trying to achieve. She kept wanting to organise it, target it, make it better.

Perhaps I've forgotten how to enjoy myself, she thought. Too much mortar fire, too many protests, too many near-death experiences. Or am I just remembering the future? Most of these happy young things would be bank clerks, factory hands, at best teachers or academics. They would screw around, they would overdose, they would try to save the whale and save the forests and save the world. Damn it, they were her parents. For a fleeting instant, she wondered if her parents *were* here, Allan and Margaret at the East Worldham pop festival.

But no. It would be too embarrassing, meeting her parents as flower children. She felt younger, diminished, just at the thought of it.

'Hey!' A woman's voice. A hand on her arm. 'Hey! I know you!'

Sam turned, saw a long face, long, grubby blonde hair. Grey-green eyes, measuring her face.

'Sam, isn't it? I'm Pippa. Remember?'

She remembered Pippa's wild talk in the cell, of the Revolution Man, and wondered if there might be a clue here.

But her cellmate from Rome had changed in eleven months: grown up, perhaps. Sam wondered what Pippa had seen – or, more important, what she'd done.

'I remember,' she told Pippa ruefully. 'How are you? When did you get out?'

Pippa shrugged. 'I can't tell you that.' But she grinned, to show it was a joke.

Sam changed tack. 'Which bands are you in to?' She didn't know much about the music, but she didn't want to trigger Pippa's paranoia.

'Bands? Oh – I'm not really here for that. We're doing some recruiting. For the TLB.' Sam raised her eyebrows. 'Total Liberation Brigade.'

'What are you liberating?'

Pippa grinned. The expression was bright and cheerful, but somehow false. 'Everything. That's why it's "total". Have a leaflet.'

The leaflet was black and red, blotchy as spilled blood. FLOWER POWER ISN'T ENOUGH – WE NEED REAL POWER, it proclaimed, in scratchy capitals. Underneath, it said, 'Changing the world needs more than wishful thinking. We need to take power and hold it for ourselves. Down with Kings and Queens, with Generals and Majors! Destroy industrialists, capitalists, imperialists!'

'I agree with you, up to a point,' said Sam, pointing at the words. 'But just moving power around from one group of people to another doesn't help. It's the systems that have to be improved.'

'We're going to improve the System,' said Pippa, somehow honouring the word with a capital S. She waved at the crowd, the field. 'It could all be like this. Peace. Love. Togetherness.'

Sam guessed that this was the line she was using with the flower children. Most of them probably believed it, at least for this afternoon. Perhaps Pippa even believed it herself. But no way could the world ever be one long festival in a summer field, with cheap drugs and free sex. Whatever the music said.

'I don't think it's that easy,' she told Pippa.

'It isn't easy, sister,' said Pippa. 'There are so many things that have to be changed first. This place is an island, an island of love in a hate-filled world. We have to remove the causes of hatred.'

'How are you going to do that? With mortar bombs?'

Pippa froze for a moment. Sam, too, froze, aware that she'd gone too far, and not quite sure why she'd done it.

'I hope not,' said Pippa at last, her eyes on the ground. 'People can be persuaded.' But her voice was empty, unconvincing, as if she'd remembered something that she'd rather forget.

Sam wanted to ask what had happened, where Pippa had lost faith in persuasion. But she'd taken enough risks in the conversation already. Instead, she tapped the leaflet and said, 'You need something better than this. Just jumping around and inciting a generalised hatred isn't enough. You need to target your campaigns.'

Pippa frowned. 'We do. We are. That's why we're here.'

Sam looked around. The crowd was denser, and the music was getting louder, warm thunder, gradual riffs, slow chords. The Doctor had vanished.

'There's going to be a demonstration later,' said Pippa suddenly.

'Against what?'

Pippa grinned again. 'Everything.' She gave Sam a swift thumbs-up. 'Must go.' And she was off across the field, leaflets under her arm, walking stiffly, like a soldier on duty.

The music got louder. Sam could feel the pull of it, the rhythm on the warmth of the afternoon, taking her away. Perhaps she did want to enjoy herself, after all. Perhaps the TARDIS was wrong, and there wasn't going to be any anomaly. Or perhaps she just deserved some time out.

She walked across the field, letting her body move to the drum beat. She saw a young man in a leather jacket looking at her, and winked. The girl with flowers in her hair was lying in the long grass by his side, her feet bare, her shirt open.

The summer of love.

Sam sashayed her way towards the stage, trying to believe in the magic, if only for a while.

The Doctor could almost smell it, the Rubasdpofiaew, the substance that the humans were calling Om-Tsor, miracle flower.

No miracle, sadly. But it was here somewhere.

Music was thudding from the stage, and the young humans were swaying in time, or slightly out of it, irregular waves of movement and feeling. The Doctor could see the mathematics of the dance, the waves, the fractals, the lines of interference. He wondered if any of the humans could see that. Some were shouting, singing along. The band was called the Brothers Sunshine – which was an irony, because clouds were drifting over the fields now, killing the heat of afternoon and leaving a chill air. It reminded the Doctor of evenings on Gaby's World, where he'd stayed for a while around his 800th birthday. Always chilly, always cloudy, on the little islands around the pole. The grey Jympyns, jelly-whales, the grey clouds, the grey sea… The Doctor shook his head, smiled at a young woman who was offering him a leaflet. Mechanically, he took it, filed it in his pocket.

He had too many memories, he decided. They overwhelmed him, forcibly taking him away from the present, immersing him in the past. He tried not to show it, for Sam's sake, because she would worry and wonder if something was wrong – and he was sure that there was nothing she could do to help. There was nothing anyone could do. It was just middle age.

It was a shame Fitz had left. He might have been able to confide in Fitz. Fitz cared about him less, and would probably understand better.

The music stopped with a sudden discordant clash that broke the Doctor's reverie. He looked up at the stage, saw the lead singer leaning into the microphone, his long hair stirring in the wind. 'Do you want a little sunshine, now?'

'Yeah!' yelled the crowd.

'Come on! Give it to me louder! We want sunshine!'

'We – want – sun – shine! We – *want – sun* – shine! *We – want –*'

And the sun came out.

The wind had changed, too. The Doctor looked up, alert, saw the clouds shifting, fast, far too fast for it to be any natural weather phenomenon. The sky was a vortex of grey and gold, the sun visible in a patch of glazed blue filled with whirling, torn shreds of cloud. There was a roaring of wind in the canopy over the stage. It was rippling, rattling against the stays that held it.

A pause. The crowd were silent, uneasy.

'We have sunshine!' said the singer. But even he seemed overawed by what had happened.

The vortex overhead split open, and a wave of black cloud rolled towards the horizon. There was a huge flare of lightning in the distance, and thunder cracked. Over the hills behind Alton, rain curtained towards the ground, gleaming grey in the sunlight. The crowd buzzed: there were some screams.

'Wow, man! That was some weather-making!' But the amplified voice sounded edgy.

The Doctor looked around the stage. His eyes were dazzled by the sun, but he caught a glimpse of a man in a chair just by the stage door. His head was back, his face turned skyward. The Doctor started towards the stage at a run, pushing his way past the bewildered people. This had to be stopped.

There was no easy way up to the stage: he had to jump over a rope, then lever himself up, clinging to the edge of the platform. He rolled on to the bare wood, jumped upright.

'Hey! Stop that!'

A heavy-set man was running towards him. The singer seemed bewildered. The Doctor dodged both of them, jumping over cables, heading for the back of the stage.

But the man in the chair was gone.

The Doctor felt a heavy hand on his shoulder. He turned, saw the heavy-set man. He smiled, of course. Smiles got you out of a lot of difficult situations.

'Get off the stage!' said the man.

'Why?' asked the Doctor innocently.

The man grinned. 'Before everyone gets the same idea. Go

on, hop it.'

'Did you see a man in a chair?' asked the Doctor.

'A chair?'

'Here. Where I'm standing. There was a man in a chair.'

The man shrugged. 'Don't think so. If there was it was probably one of the stage hands.' His hand tightened on the Doctor's arm, pulling him towards the back of the stage – which was just where the Doctor wanted to go.

There was a noise from the crowd at that moment, an unbelieving noise, a whistling of breath. And the light had changed – it was slightly whiter. As if –

The Doctor glanced up, saw only the canvas canopy above the stage. He broke free of the security man, ran back across the stage, jumped down, then looked up again.

A circle of white cloud had formed, high in the sky, like the contrail of a spaceship. As the Doctor watched, the circle filled with more cloud, quite slowly, as if a pastel artist were painting on the stratosphere. A capital R formed, and two arrow heads were made on the circle. It began to drift, to blur slowly. Faint rainbow colours formed, as the sun caught falling ice crystals.

It was the same symbol that Sam had described on the embassy in Italy. But the Doctor had seen it more recently than that. In fact –

He looked down, at the leaflet in his hand. The symbol was there, in red, above the words FLOWER POWER ISN'T ENOUGH – WE NEED REAL POWER.

Above his head, the new white clouds were turning pink, as if they were being polluted with blood.

'The same one?' The Doctor's face was earnest, excited,

serious, all at once. The light was fading, the music was back, fast and discordant, the lights on the stage angry. But the crowd were still a little subdued. It hadn't been difficult for the Doctor and Sam to find a quiet space to talk. 'The woman you met in Italy?'

'Yes. She talked about a "Revolution Man" then.'

The Doctor nodded, jerkily. 'It was a man I saw on stage.'

'You don't know that he was anything to do with it.'

She remembered that once, she wouldn't have risked contradicting the Doctor. Now, she did it all the time.

He glanced at her, shrugged. 'Call it a feeling.'

'I think we should track down Pippa.' She glanced around, looking for the head of grubby blonde hair in the crowd. Red light was crawling out from the stage, making it hard to see anything. 'She knows something.'

'Why? What did she say?'

Sam shrugged back at the Doctor. 'Call it a feeling.'

They both smiled.

'You take Pippa, then,' he said. 'I'll take the Brothers Sunshine.'

He found them in a green-and-white caravan in an upper field reserved for the musicians. They were both long-haired, with dark trousers and dark jackets. They looked smaller, more real, than they had on stage, their strangely similar, contemplative faces pale in the half-dark inside the caravan. A guitar was leaning against the lower bunk; otherwise the cramped space could have been any caravan, anywhere: twin bunks with a folding ladder, plywood doors with wooden knobs, jackets slung on hooks, a tartan thermos flask on a stainless steel draining board. There was little of the glamour of stardom here.

The Doctor looked around, and from the corner of an eye watched the brothers watching him.

'Who did you say you were from?' said the taller one at last.

'United Nations Intelligence Taskforce. It's a new –'

'We don't *deal* with that bullshit, man,' said the smaller, darker, brother. 'That's an order of things that's passed away. You understand? What you saw was the new order, and if you can't be with it that's your problem.'

The Doctor stared at the man for a moment. The anger was genuine: there was no doubt of that. The man's respiratory rate was up, his pupils had narrowed. His eyes were puffy, red, as if he'd been crying: the Doctor wondered what had triggered the allergy. 'Weren't you just a little bit afraid of what happened?' he asked.

The taller brother replied. 'No, we weren't. *You* were afraid because you tried to understand it. To explain it away. But you can't explain away what happens when you change things. Change is a miracle, it just happens.'

'No,' said the Doctor, 'I don't think so. People can make change happen. And what happened out there certainly wasn't a miracle. It has an explanation.'

'Perhaps. But not the sort of explanation you "understand".'

'You'll find out,' hinted the darker one.

A pause. The Doctor became aware of a clock, ticking loudly. A reminder that time was running out.

'You're not going to tell me, then?' he asked them.

The taller one shrugged. The other one stood up, began fiddling with the thermos.

The Doctor stood up too. He could feel the anger building up. He decided it was time to call the brothers' bluff.

'Because this is serious,' he snapped. 'It isn't a game, an afternoon of mystical chairs to pull in a bigger audience for your next gig. The substance that drew your sign in the sky was a deadly weapon. In the wrong hands it could put everyone on Earth in danger.'

'That's probably true,' said the taller brother. 'But you're the "wrong hands". Not us. And, until you know why that is, you'll be part of the problem.'

The Doctor looked from one brother to another, and began to work out where the magic of the sixties had gone. There was no love in here, there were no flowers. Just wishful thinking fast turning sour, into paranoia and hatred.

'What a shame,' he said aloud. 'I wonder why it always has to be this way.'

But that didn't work either: the brothers remained silent, glowering and cynical. The clock ticked. The Doctor turned and left, closing the tinny door of the caravan behind him.

Pippa wasn't alone when Sam found her. She was sitting in a circle with four other people, all men. Sam watched the tension in their bodies, the anger on their faces, and decided that these weren't potential converts, but Pippa's friends. The already converted; the already angry.

'Er... hello,' she said, cautiously, touching Pippa on the shoulder.

The young woman glanced up. 'Hi!' Her face broke into that bright, false smile. 'What did you think of the Brothers?'

'D'you mean the music or the air display?'

Pippa hesitated, then grinned. 'Both.'

'Powerful stuff.' Beat. 'Both.'

Pippa nodded, then abruptly waved at the rest of the

group. 'These are Mike –' a tall, glowering man in a brown leather jacket – 'Jim, Craig.'

Craig was blonde and curly-haired: he smiled and said, 'Hi, how are you?' with an American twang. It sounded genuine.

'And this is Josh,' finished Pippa.

Josh was dark-skinned, and dressed smartly – Sam guessed that he was African. He gave a polite smile and a nod, but he wasn't like the others. Sam remembered the racism of the sixties, and decided he was probably an outsider even here among the so-called flower children. Most likely he'd fallen in with this group for no better reason than that they would talk to him.

She sat down with them, politely refusing the offer of a drag on a cigarette that was being passed around. She knew she would have to keep a clear head in the conversation that followed: whatever was in the cigarette wasn't likely to help. She accepted a coloured tablet, but palmed it, mimed swallowing motions.

The conversation continued, drifting, rudderless, exchanges about the music, about other festivals, fragments of sentences that didn't seem to go anywhere: Sam joined in as little as she could, and when she did contrived to sound innocent about the music scene as an excuse for her relative ignorance. She was surprised at the significance given to bands she'd never heard of: the Blueberries, the Magic Windows, the Clever Freddies. Bands that had been liked, but had never quite made it to the charts. In the darkness, with the music thudding behind the voices, the bands seemed more interesting, more alive, than the well-known ones.

'Why do you wear your hair so short?' asked Pippa at one point, when the guys had got up to dance.

'Where I come from...' began Sam, then let the sentence trail off.

But Pippa wasn't letting go. 'And where do you "come from"?'

Sam didn't reply. She wondered again what Pippa knew.

'I don't mind if you're a dyke,' said Pippa. 'Some of the guys might, though.'

So much for freedom of the mind, thought Sam. If I wear my hair short it means, first, that I'm a lesbian, and second, that this might be a problem. For the second time that day she was aware of just how far the flower children had to go before they reached maturity. Most of them – she recalled again her parents' generation – would never make it. On the other hand, the steps they had taken would make it possible for future generations to be better than they had been.

'You want to join us, don't you?' asked Pippa suddenly, her voice loud against a silence from the stage.

A voice spoke over the PA, giving Sam an excuse to keep quiet for a few seconds. When it stopped, she said, 'I'd like to try. I'm not sure what you do, though.'

'We make signs. Like the one you saw earlier.'

Sam felt her heart beat faster. This was the information she was after.

'*You* did that?'

'Not me.'

'Then who did?' Sam made the question sound as wide-eyed and innocuous as possible.

'You know I can't tell you. Not now.' Pippa glanced over her shoulder, a quick, nervous, spy's movement. 'The guys are coming back. I'll talk to them. Go and dance for a bit.'

Sam hesitated, tried to read her companion's face in the

115

half-light. She thought she saw anger there, maybe suspicion.

Keeping her own expression friendly, and a little bewildered, she shuffled away and into the crowd around the stage. The music was quiet, and couples were dancing slowly. Sam slouched near the stage, avoiding the hopeful glances of several single guys on the perimeter.

Then she realised that one of them was the Doctor. He walked up to her, and presented her with a carnation.

'Shall we dance?'

Sam glanced at the other couples smooching, and wondered about it, but the Doctor had already taken her hands. He began to waltz her across the trodden mud as if it were a parquet dance floor, avoiding the other couples with smart changes of footing. Sam found it hard to keep up.

'The Brothers Sunshine know, but won't tell us,' he said. 'What about our anarchist friends?'

'The same. But I think they might offer me membership.'

'Hmm. Well, I can't join the Brothers Sunshine. Do you want to try it?'

'Haven't much choice, have I?' She smiled up at him.

He smiled back, released her, and bowed. Sam returned with a gentle curtsy, resisting the urge to thumb her nose at him. Then she turned and walked away quickly.

Pippa's group had moved on: the patch of ground was empty, apart from a few pale cigarette stubs. Sam followed a hunch and made her way towards the entrance gate. Pippa was waiting.

'We're going now,' she said simply. 'They're at the van. You can come if you want to.'

'Where are we going?'

'More sign painting,' said Pippa. Sam must have let a flicker

116

of a frown show on her face, because Pippa quickly added, 'Nothing dangerous.'

Sam wondered what the group did that was dangerous. She remembered the sign in the sky, the sign carved into the front of the Rome embassy. It was quite possible that one of the guys she'd been chatting music with was the Revolution Man, murderer of hundreds of people. Or even that Pippa was. Was this worth the risk?

She could see the van ahead now. The lights were on, the engine revving. Clouds of filthy diesel fumes misted the air.

'Come on, Pips!' Craig's voice. It had gained a leader-like impatience and authority. Pippa took Sam's hand, and all but dragged her through the open back doors. Craig and Mike were sitting cross-legged on a carpeted floor, between roped-up cans of paint. Jim was driving, and a man Sam didn't know was sitting next to him in the front passenger seat. Josh had gone.

They set off along the rough track towards the road, the suspension creaking. Sam found a grab handle, a simple metal loop welded to the wall of the van, and held on the best she could.

'Where *are* we going?' she whispered to Pippa, again.

The young woman exchanged a glance with Craig, who nodded.

'The American Embassy,' she said, then giggled. 'We're going to finish it off!'

Chapter Nine

White. The brilliant white of ice, jagged rocks, sheer slopes towering into the deep blue sky. They called these mountains the roof of the world, and Maddie could see why. The Himalayas seemed to float above the tops of the trees, as if the forest continued underneath them, a carpet in the house of the gods. The path she was walking was irrelevant, a thread in the carpet which vanished into the greenery ahead.

Maddie thought of the Himalayan gods walking their own vast paths through the ice fields, pictured them stumbling, falling… She felt a moment of pure white panic, and had to stop walking and close her eyes. She felt a touch on her arm, opened her eyes, saw Fitz looking at her with concern. He slipped an arm round her, clumsy in their thick jackets.

'We don't have to do this,' he said. 'We could just go back to Kathmandu. I spoke to the driver – the bus will be back in an hour.'

'No.' Her voice was firmer than she'd intended, almost a rebuke for cowardice, which wasn't fair. She snuggled her head against Fitz's shoulder, to make up for it. After a moment like that, they walked on, their boots crunching on the loose stone surface of the track.

It had been much further than either of them had expected from Kathmandu. The bus had been slow and crowded. There didn't seem to be many Westerners on this particular trail, and Maddie had several times wondered if they had the right village after all. She'd looked at the crammed seats, the laughing young men sitting cross-legged in the aisle, and thought of the crowded railway carriages, with people clinging to the roofs and the windows, falling, falling. She'd been very glad when at last the driver had stopped and shouted, 'Ghumding!'

She wondered when finding the truth about Om-Tsor had changed from a concern to an obsession. At first, all she'd wanted to do was forget it – all of it. She hadn't even wanted to see Fitz. But he'd visited every day, and when she was out of hospital he'd insisted on buying her a drink, then a meal. He was fun, with his incredible tales of space and time travel, his alien accents, his juggling tricks. OK, so he was poor, surviving on the interest from bonds left him by his mysterious friend the Doctor, but he wasn't a bad guitarist, and could play Stones and Beatles songs. And he was far less demanding and strange than Ed.

Sometimes she thought of Ed, of the vanishing trick that had been his death, the ruined concert hall. What had he said that morning? 'There are things you don't want to know about.' What had he known? Why had the Asian man tried to kill her – had she just been in the way? Or was it to do with the train, or with her use of Om-Tsor?

She'd talked about it to Fitz. At first, he'd tried to help. Then he'd tried to make her forget it. Finally he too had become obsessed with finding the answers, if only for her sake.

The police had been unhelpful: they'd never found any clues about the attacker, and despite Maddie's story they were suspicious of Fitz, probably because of his half-German ancestry. So Maddie and Fitz had tried contacting the other members of the band. Rick Davis and Mike Perrin were still performing, as the Brothers Sunshine. She'd met them in a bar in the East End: long-faced, long-haired, and oddly dark for sunshine brothers, they'd talked about music for an hour, but they both claimed they knew nothing about any Om-Tsor drug.

'Ed was into some weird things,' one of them had said.

Ron Turton, the guitarist, had been different. They'd found him in a dirty bed-sit south of the river. Pale, emaciated, his bare arms covered with sores, he'd watched them with huge eyes as Maddie told her part of the story.

'I should have stopped him,' he said, when she'd finished. 'He took it. I knew he would – he was greedy.'

'Took it?'

'In Nepal. There were these monks in the village. He was talking to the young one for ages, said he'd taken this stuff. I thought it was hash. Then he said he could move mountains, be a god, that sort of thing. I should have stopped him then. But I didn't believe it. I didn't believe it until that roof came off – Christ!'

He'd gone on for some time, rambling from London to Kathmandu and back again, via stories about his childhood in the country, but neither Maddie nor Fitz had been able to get much in the way of definite information. He could remember the name of the village in Nepal where Ed had found the drug – Ghumding – but he wasn't sure whether the monks had a monastery there or were just passing through. He didn't know which religious order they belonged to, though he thought they might have been Tibetans, exiled after the Chinese invasion.

Fitz and Maddie had talked all the way back to Fitz's bed-sit, and then half the night after that. They'd concluded that there was only one possible way to find out the truth about

Om-Tsor – go to Nepal and find the monks. They cashed in some of Fitz's bonds and bought tickets to Kathmandu.

A touch on Maddie's arm brought her back to the present, to the forest trail and the sharp smell of ice.

'There!' Fitz was pointing ahead, and Maddie could see a gap in the trees, the pale-green, mud-streaked surface of fields, the corner of a stone building. She glanced at his face, saw a shadow of worry there, perhaps even fear.

He caught her looking, and smiled, squeezed her arm.

Perhaps, she thought, it had been Fitz who had wanted to go back to Kathmandu. Perhaps she should have gone back, for his sake. He'd come halfway round the world to find out who'd killed her ex-boyfriend. And tried to kill her. Fitz said that he'd left the Doctor because he'd had enough adventure and danger to last a lifetime. But now here he was, getting involved in adventure – perhaps even danger – again. He could have said no. He could have been more determined in his attempts to persuade Maddie to put the experience behind her. He could have got a sensible job, proposed...

Maddie grinned. She would have left him if he'd done that. And he probably knew it.

By the time they reached the fields around the village, the light was fading and Maddie's backpack was digging hard into her shoulders. There seemed to be no one around, only a few shadowy figures working in the terraces that climbed the side of the valley. There was still no sign of anything that resembled a monastery, even a temporary one. The buildings were low, wooden-roofed, clustered around an open space of beaten earth and grubby stone. Two small children in dun-coloured costumes looked up at Maddie and Fitz with big eyes.

'We're looking for the monks,' said Fitz slowly.

The children looked at each other. Maddie guessed they were both about eight. '*Sheesh?*' asked one.

Fitz frowned. Maddie reached into her pocket, found a few small coins. The children eagerly extended their hands. She pressed a single coin into each. 'Lama?' she asked.

The shorter of the two jabbered a long stream of syllables accompanied by much vigorous pointing in several directions. Maddie gave him another coin. He ran off, yelling over his shoulder at them.

They followed the child down several narrow, stone-walled alleys that smelled strongly of animal dung. At last they reached an old stone barn, its roof patched, windowless, its door no more than a loose cloth hanging over a gap in the stone.

'Lama,' confirmed the child, extending his palm once more. Maddie put her remaining two coins into it. Fitz was already advancing towards the building, wearing the slightly insolent expression he seemed to use whenever he wasn't quite sure what he was walking into. Maddie followed quickly, wishing he wouldn't assume that only he could cope. He might claim to have travelled in time and met aliens, but she was the one who'd been nearly killed. For some reason, that had made her less afraid.

She pushed her way through the cloth hanging behind him. It stank of stale milk and earth. Inside, it was too dark to see anything for a moment. Then Maddie saw a pale shape near one wall. After a moment she realised that it was a man, wearing a saffron-coloured robe.

He was muttering something over and over again. A mantra? There was a faint tick of beads, as regular as the sound of a clock. Fitz spoke, briefly and awkwardly. He'd learned a tourist's Nepali and Hindi, both of which had proved all but useless except with officials, and it wasn't any different here. The old man – he must be old, surely – just kept up his mantra, and the beads kept ticking.

Maddie became aware of a faint smell of candle wax over the dung and stale milk. And another, ranker, smell. She realised, quite suddenly, that there was a goat only about three feet in front of her, pale and curl-horned, one of its bulging eyes turned to her. It pawed the ground as Maddie took a step back, but it must have been tethered, or tame, because it made no other move to approach her.

Light shifted around them: Maddie heard a footstep behind her and turned quickly. A young man in a costume of battered brown leather faced them. He smiled – a wide, toothy, innocuous grin.

'You are looking for lama?' Maddie nodded. 'I am the one lama. I and Shambala.'

Maddie nodded again.

'No monastery?'

The young man gestured around him, smiled. 'This is the monastery. This only. Until we return.'

'Return?'

'To Tibet. We leave Tibet nineteen fifty-nine. Chinese. You know?'

Maddie knew. Tibet had been occupied by Chinese forces for seventeen years. No one was allowed in any more. In Kathmandu she and Fitz had been told that the hippie trail stopped at the border – the few who'd tried to cross had been politely turned back. She had heard that these monks had been exiled from Tibet: what she hadn't realised was what that meant – living in poverty in a goat shed in an obscure village hiding under the roof of the world.

'But I have yet to offer you tea!' exclaimed the young man, clapping his hands. 'Wait. I will boil billy.'

For a crazy moment Maddie thought he meant he was going to cook the goat. She started to protest, then saw the lama produce a battered tin kettle. He filled it with water from a bucket and went outside.

'I hope the goat hasn't been drinking from the bucket,' whispered Maddie.

'Or contributing to it,' said Fitz, grinning.

She nudged him. 'Oh, shut up!'

They followed their host back through the smelly doorway, saw him placing the kettle in a cradle over a fire smouldering in the cold, damp space between the barn and a stone wall.

He straightened. 'It will not be very long,' he said. Despite his apologetic tone his eyes were sharp, examining both of them. 'Why you to see lama?' he asked.

'We were curious about your history,' asked Fitz. 'Where was your monastery in Tibet?'

'Om-Tsor,' said the monk with a smile.

Maddie felt her heart thudding hard. There could be no doubt, now, that this was the right place. 'Where's Om-Tsor?' she asked.

'Very high valley.' The monk's smile was still fixed, like a mask, but his eyes were growing wary. 'I cannot say too much. The Chinese are in our land now. I cannot tell too much to strangers. I am sorry to seem distrustful, but words spread like steam from kettle.' He gestured at the fire, and his grin broadened. The kettle, in fact, wasn't steaming very much.

'We need to know about –' began Fitz.

'No we don't,' said Maddie quickly, putting a hand on his arm. Lines formed on the lama's face, making him look older than Maddie had first guessed – perhaps in his late thirties. His hand had moved near his waist, in an ominously defensive gesture. There was a scabbard there, a scruffy leather affair. It didn't hide the wooden handle of a knife.

The monk saw where she was looking, and sighed. 'I am sorry. We must be careful.'

Maddie was thinking of Kathmandu, of the questions they'd asked there about Tibetan monks, even about Om-Tsor. The words had already spread. Had either of them mentioned the name of the village? Probably. That was what they'd been trying to confirm, after all.

She looked up, over the wall at the Himalayas. They were grey, like faded steel.

The kettle boiled at last. Their host went into the shed-monastery and produced three tin cups. He poured from the kettle, which must have contained tea, since the fluid was thick and brown. The lama added some thick, curded milk from a jug, and some raw-looking sugar from a pouch.

The resultant fluid stank, and Maddie could hardly bring herself to drink it. Fitz visibly paled, but bravely took a large gulp.

'Now we introduce ourselves,' said the monk. 'I am King George. It is not my real name but will do for us to talk.' Fitz and Maddie exchanged a glance, then quickly introduced themselves before they could start giggling.

The three of them sipped tea in silence for a few moments after that. The wind breathed cold air over their faces.

Finally Maddie said, 'We need to be honest. We've come a

long way to speak to you, and I have to tell you the truth. A friend of ours took something from you, and he's died as a result. I was nearly killed.'

King George nodded. 'I thought it was like that. We have suffered this too. Four of us died, and some others were taken back to China. When your friend took… what he took, he was foolish and greedy.'

Maddie nodded. 'I know.'

'So why are you here? You live in England, yes? You are safe there.'

'No we're not,' snapped Fitz. 'That's where the killings happened.'

The lama got up abruptly, walked into the shed. They heard him speaking in another language, rapidly, heard a few soft replies.

When he came out, King George wasn't smiling any more. 'It has been used. It is still being used.' He sat down, cross-legged, on the bare dirt, and looked down at his knees. 'I will tell you everything I know.'

'There was a very high valley in the Roof of the World, where ice reigned as eternal Lord, and the only sounds were the wind searing the rocks and the creak of the ice river as it moved. The valley was on no road, it led to no pass over the mountains, and so no one went there, except perhaps the occasional lost traveller – and all of those died.

'Then, some centuries ago, the Manchu Chinese came to Tibet as rulers. Just as in our time many lamas were exiled from Lhasa. One group from the lamasery of the Silver Monkey lost their way among the mountains. Their leader, who we will call Hin-Dali, decided that their path had ended and they must die. He told the lamas that they had been led to the high mountains to reach nirvana. So they sat down at the base of the ice river, in the most beautiful place, and awaited their end.

'Then they saw a mist! Imagine their feelings, when they saw a mist above the ice – and smelled the air of growing things, of soil! Hin-Dali feared an illusion, and was reluctant to let anyone seek the source of this miracle, but some of the younger monks were eager to live, and they went anyway.

'And so they found the valley, and found in it a place between three tall stones, where the earth was warm and small flowers grew. They called it Om-Tsor, which in their dialect meant the Miracle Flower.

'Perhaps they ate the flowers because they were hungry – there can have been little enough for them to eat. Anyway, they ate them. And they found that they could walk tall, tall among the mountains as if they were of the mountains themselves. They could move rocks the size of a house, carve the great river of ice, and if they breathed on the land it was a warm wind, as if they had become gods and could make the winds their own.

'They could have used the power to make revenge on their enemies in Lhasa but Hin-Dali insisted that they should take this gift of life and use it to make a garden from the valley.

'So, as godlike men, they scooped away the ice and smoothed the rock, and brought soil from distant forests, and seeds. As men, they tilled the soil and planted the seeds and built shelters. Then each one would take turns to be a god-man and guard the valley from storms, and breathe warm air on it, and bring warm water to it, so that the crops would grow and the monks could live. And the most important crop of all was the tiny flower, the Miracle Flower, whose petals made men into gods.

'Thus Om-Tsor became the highest lamasery on Earth, the highest holy place on Earth, the highest place where men could live.'

'And what happened?' asked Maddie after a while.

'When the Chinese came in nineteen fifty-one, they didn't even know we were there. But in nineteen fifty-nine, when there was the "crackdown" and the Dali Lama left, they found us. They threw us out of our monastery, and we had to leave the valley.'

'And the Om-Tsor?'

'We burned the plants. People such as those who found us should not have such power. That is why we came here, rather than go with the Dali Lama and the others to exile in India. We did not want anyone to know.'

'And now they do,' said Fitz. He was standing up, peering around as if looking for enemies. Maddie wanted to pull him back down to ground level.

King George gave a shrug. 'Well, we have little enough of Om-Tsor – your friend took most of it. Shambala watches with the rest. But it will soon be gone, and the flowers are burned. Those who killed your friend only imagined they could find power.'

'Ed had a lot left. It was taken.'

The monk clasped his hands and bowed slightly. 'Then that is the fate of Om-Tsor: that the last of it should be used for evil.' His smile returned. 'Don't worry, there isn't very much.'

Maddie frowned. There had, in fact, been quite a lot. And judging by what had happened with just a couple of flakes…

Fitz, too, was evidently puzzled. 'That's not what the Doctor said. He was worried.' He sat down. 'And so were you, a minute ago.'

King George looked away, then stood up and shuffled to the fire. For the first time Maddie noticed that he was wearing something that looked like an old pair of bedroom slippers on his feet.

'More tea?' he asked.

Maddie politely accepted, and motioned Fitz to do the same. The tea poured thick and black now, and was even more disgusting when mixed with the goat's milk and raw sugar. When they had taken the ritual first sip and were sitting down again, Maddie caught the lama's eye and said gently, 'We do need the truth. I know how much Om-Tsor was taken.' She remembered the near-empty box, her sense of panic.

'You want the truth? You are sure?'

Maddie nodded, felt Fitz take her hand.

The lama looked at the earth again, and clasped his hands together.

'The truth is, probably, the end of the world.'

Chapter Ten

'Are we clear on the mission?' Craig's American accent was discernible even though he was whispering. 'Do we all know our roles here?'

Pippa and Sam glanced at each other and smiled. Pippa put her lips near to Sam's ear and whispered, 'Never stops, does he?'

Sam rolled her eyes. Once it had become clear that Sam was to be admitted to the group's secrets, Craig had done little but talk all the long, bumpy way from Alton to London. The idea for this 'mission' had been his, apparently. They were going to paint the embassy 'red with blood', using cans of signal-red acrylic.

The night was quiet, and fairly warm, which was bad: even though it was 5 a.m., they had met several drunken partygoers as they made their way towards St James's square. Worse, one of the embassies – not the American – seemed to be holding an all-night ball. Cars came and went under the trees, amber street light glinting off their darkened windows. Sam saw them stop on the far side of the square and pick up men in suits and women in evening dresses – guarded, no doubt, by men with discreet guns.

'Told you we should have gone in togs.' Jim, the group's only genuine working-class member, said. He'd suggested they hire suits, so as to blend with anyone who might be around in London's diplomatic district in the middle of the night. The others had laughed at the idea. Now it was beginning to look as if he'd been right. They were going to be very conspicuous in their jeans and shirts, straight from the festival.

'Perhaps we should have worn kaftans,' suggested Sam. Pippa giggled. The three men in the group just glanced at each other.

'OK,' said Craig. 'We may have to do a change of plan here. We'll go down this side.'

Sam had no idea what he was talking about, but before she could ask Craig had walked off along the wrong side of the square, towards the Embassy that was holding the ball. The three other men followed, like soldiers on parade.

Pippa frowned at Sam, who shrugged and set off after them. The paint cans clanked in her rucksack as she turned the corner. She saw Craig kneel and take out his supply of paint, pull off the lids. The two other men did the same.

Sam nudged Pippa. 'Who are we hitting? These aren't Americans.' She could see Asian faces among the dignitaries getting into their cars.

'Doesn't matter. The publicity will be good.'

Sam said nothing. She was beginning to wonder about the Total Liberation Brigade. They seemed too amateurish to bring in good publicity for anarchy, or anything else. This random change of target could easily be a hideous mistake. She just hoped that the embassy wasn't Chinese.

Everyone had their paint out now, except Pippa, who was hopping from foot to foot, her short blonde hair bobbing. 'What if –'

Too late. Craig was already running forward, shouting at the top of his voice. 'Free the mind! Free the spirit!' He hurled a can of paint at the nearest car. It missed, and rolled on the road, spilling a dark stain.

Somebody was pointing a gun at Craig, somebody else was shouting orders. An Asian man in a suit dived for cover.

Sam put a hand on Jim's shoulder. 'This could get dodgy,' she said. 'Stay here. We've probably done enough.'

But there was no stopping the other three. They charged after Craig, hurled paint cans into the air. One crashed into the car, pouring fluorescent red paint all over the gleaming black.

Sam heard the distinctive thud of a silenced pistol.

'Everyone back!' she yelled. No one took any notice.

Of course. They were men. Sam still couldn't get used to the fact that men took no notice of anything that a woman said in this era.

Now Pippa was running forward. Sam had no idea why. She looked around for weapons, saw one policeman with a light pistol, crouching behind the bonnet of the car. Everyone else was on the floor.

'It's only paint!' shouted Pippa, her voice quavery with hysteria. 'It's only freedom!'

It didn't make much sense, but it seemed to work. A clinical part of Sam's mind noted that Pippa had performed the correct role for a woman in this period: showing fear in the face of violence. Therefore she'd been listened to. Craig and the others were pulling back, and the diplomats were cautiously sitting up. One of them was speckled with the red paint. It looked like blood. Sam shuddered.

'Long live anarchy!' bawled Craig.

'You nearly didn't live at all, you bloody fools!' snapped someone from the direction of the embassy – perhaps the detective with the gun. He said something else, about arrest, but Sam was already running.

She got ahead of the others – probably they didn't run as a regular thing. Sam paced it, not panicking, jogging evenly. She turned, saw Pippa gasping some way behind her, but no sign of official pursuit.

She stopped, waited. Pippa caught up, then Craig, then Mike.

There was no sign of Jim.

They waited for ten minutes, leaning against one of the huge white monuments of London, watching the stars, the empty street, anything but each other's face.

At last Craig said, 'I think they've got him. What do we do now?'

Fitz woke to the sound of dogs barking. The sound had a curious echo to it: flat, but long, as if the sound was being played back on a tape recorder at the wrong speed. He sat up, felt the cold air hit his face. It quickly seeped into his body, even though he'd slept in one of his sweaters. Maddie was already up: her sleeping bag was empty, and her boots, trousers and coat were gone from the chair.

'The end of the world.' Fitz remembered the lama's smiling face. Surely it couldn't be that bad. He looked at the bare stone walls of the tiny room. He could still smell the goat in the barn below, and his stomach grumbled at the memory of the tea and the thought that there would probably be more of it for breakfast. If he hadn't seen what Om-Tsor could do – if he hadn't travelled with the Doctor – he wouldn't have believed a word of it.

Maddie came in through the narrow, curtained doorway, and glanced at him brightly. 'Know what time it is?'

Fitz shrugged. 'Ten o'clock?'

She grinned. 'Half past seven. But King George and Shambala were out milking goats at six.' She stretched. 'It's a beautiful day.'

Fitz wriggled out of the sleeping bag, pulled on his trousers, his second sweater and his coat. None of this made him feel any warmer. He looked out of the tiny window cut into the roof, saw grey mountains, pale fields.

'We're going to need the Doctor,' he said.

'Why? Have you got a sore throat?'

'You know who I mean.'

'Yes. And you know I don't agree with you.' Her voice had become tight, petulant.

'That was different. That was London. We're nearer now.'

No reply. He turned to her. She was rolling up her sleeping bag, not looking at him.

'I wasn't dreaming, Maddie. We did travel in time and space. How do you think I knew all about Om-Tsor?' Still no reply. The sleeping bag thudded on the floor; the straps squeaked as she rolled it up and tied it. 'I brought the card with me.'

He'd found it in his pocket, that day in the hospital. A dark-blue card with white writing and a strange sense of… *depth* to it. PUBLIC CALL BOX, it said. PRESS TO CALL. There was a button, like a small, white, hatched window. Fitz had sewn the card into the bottom of his rucksack, under an extra flap of cloth.

He was almost sure it would work.

Maddie was shouldering her rucksack with the sleeping bag strapped on top. The arrangement was clumsy, and she staggered for a moment. Fitz caught her arm, but she shrugged it off. They went down the steps in silence into the goaty warmth of the barn. There was no rail: the steps were cut into the thick stone wall. Maddie leaned against it, but refused Fitz's offer of a hand.

Shambala, the old man, was sitting cross-legged in his usual place. His faded robes made him look strangely like a flower, an autumn crocus amid the piles of straw and neat racks of agricultural tools. He was fiddling with a small mechanical device, perhaps a prayer wheel.

'I can't rely on your friend, Fitz,' said Maddie suddenly. 'I know he saved my life. I can remember… something. But you can't expect me to trust a bit of plastic with a crazy picture on it. I don't know anything about "the Doctor". If he can travel in space and time, perhaps he brought Om-Tsor here in the first place.'

'That's impossible,' said Fitz flatly.

'Is it?'

Fitz realised he wasn't sure. The Doctor wouldn't have done such a thing deliberately – but he had seemed a bit slapdash sometimes. And how long had he lived? More than a thousand years, he'd said. Then there was the TARDIS – a being in its own right, if the Doctor was to be believed, and utterly alien. Could any of them trust that?

The curtain at the end of the barn flapped and King George came in. He wasn't smiling, and his eyes were darting, wild.

Fitz noticed that the dogs were barking again, this time in a frenzy. As if –

'There is trouble,' said King George.

Fitz could hear engines now, the creak and judder of heavy machines moving on the half-surfaced road.

'Go on!' hissed King George. 'Hide!'

Maddie shook her head, but Fitz was already scanning the

barn, looking for good places. There weren't any: nothing except a few piles of straw.

The old man was moving, shoving the prayer wheel out of sight under his robes. King George lifted a long, straight horn with a bell-shaped end which was propped against the back wall beside the steps. With a movement that managed to be both reverential and quick, he laid it down flat and began to throw more straw over it.

'Hide!' he urged again.

'What is it?' asked Maddie.

Fitz couldn't believe she was so slow on the uptake.

'Army,' said the lama.

'Armoured cars, I should think,' said Fitz.

'*What?*'

Outside, the engines stopped. Someone was shouting, and the language didn't sound like Nepali. It sounded Chinese. Surely the Chinese couldn't just send an army unit into Nepal. But the two lamas' obvious fear, and the expression of consternation on King George's face –

'*Hide!*'

Maddie was going back up the steps, which was no use at all. It wasn't as if there was a wardrobe in the tiny cell. Then Fitz remembered that his pack and sleeping bag were still up there, and started after her. If they found that, with all his notes on Om-Tsor...

The shouting outside was louder, and the dogs were still barking. Above him, he could hear Maddie shuffling about in the room. His backpack appeared through the curtain: he grabbed it quickly, looked around the barn once more. There had to be somewhere he could hide. But would it work? It might be better to bluff it out. The old thrill, of danger, of fear, uncertainty was clutching his gut. It was as if even *thinking* of calling the Doctor had summoned all the usual danger that surrounded him.

Outside there was a thud, and an animal squeal of pain which ended in a gurgle. After a second Fitz realised that the thud had been a gunshot.

Two words, rapped out. Then footsteps, running footsteps with a military rhythm and power. The curtain was flung back.

The man was wearing what seemed to be a Nepalese uniform, but he spoke in Chinese. Fitz struggled to piece together a meaning from his limited knowledge of Mandarin, but the accent wasn't familiar.

Without any warning, King George screamed and rushed forward. Fitz opened his mouth to shout, but didn't see the knife until it was embedded in the soldier's throat.

Now they'll kill us, he thought.

The soldier crumpled on to the floor with an expression of anger and astonishment on his face. He struggled to pull the knife out, then died. Blood soaked his tunic, red on green.

There was another soldier in the doorway. He grabbed the lama, dragged him upright, threw him out through the tattered curtain. Outside, there was a grunt and scream. The second soldier gestured at Fitz, who jumped to the ground from the steps.

The sudden movement was too much. A bullet splintered stone next to Fitz's knee. Shaking, he very slowly put his hands on his head and, equally slowly, crouched down. The soldier approached him. Fitz kept his eyes on the floor. Outside there was an irregular thudding which might be boots hitting flesh.

'I'm English,' said Fitz. 'Shoot me and there will be trouble.'

It didn't sound as convincing as David Niven. His voice was shaking, which didn't help.

Boots stopped in front of him. Clean, but worn leather. Dark. Perhaps they would be the last thing he would ever see.

Hands grabbed his shoulders, and he was jolted upright. A soldier ran past him, up the steps. How many of them were there? He saw the old lama being lifted by two soldiers, felt a wrench at his shoulders. He was being dragged out of the barn, his boots scraping on the floor.

Upstairs, Maddie gave a muffled shout. There was a thud. Fitz shouted, felt his head jerked sideways. His vision blurred, and lights danced in front of his eyes.

Headlights. He was outside, breathing cold, cold air, his cheeks hot. Engines were starting.

'Maddie?' he asked. His voice sounded blurred. There was a metal door, a dark space behind it. He was tumbling in. A sharp pain in his side. The old lama was bundled in after him. Fitz struggled to sit up, but bolts of pain moved down his back. The door slammed and they were moving, the car lurching from side to side, flinging Fitz painfully against the metal.

'Maddie!'

There was light of a sort, a slit in the armour. With an effort, Fitz sat up and peered through. He saw nothing but blue sky, with flickers of grey that might have been clouds or mountains.

But there could be no doubt where they were going.

'Tibet,' he said to the old man. 'We're going to Tibet.'

The man said nothing. He hadn't spoken to either Fitz or

Maddie since they'd arrived: Fitz assumed he knew no English.

'They'll be looking for Om-Tsor,' said Fitz. 'You mustn't tell them where the valley is.' Though he doubted that either of the lamas would talk.

He looked at his companion, saw that he was slumped back against the metal. There was a dark stain on the chest of his robe. His eyes were open, but they were blank, glazed.

Slowly, Fitz realised that the man was dead.

Chapter Eleven

The Total Liberation Brigade had a house in East Cheam, an ordinary Victorian end-terrace with smoke-blackened bricks. They'd daubed their symbol – the Revolution Man's symbol – on the bricks, and painted the door and window frames red. Some of the red ran down the walls. It wasn't like blood – too pale and watery – but Sam was sure that the effect was intentional. She wondered how a real flower child would react to this not very subtle Goth-horror imagery. She decided to opt for a few nervous looks.

Inside, the place was empty. As the others looked for Jim, Sam followed along and got a guided tour of rooms with paint-daubed walls, filled with paint-daubed vinyl furniture. More paint had pooled on bare floorboards. Here and there was a scruffy rug. The place smelled: of old dinners, of dust, and, inevitably, of paint.

Somebody put a record player on: it was dull and tinny, and the sound was distorted. It bleated out a twanging, architectural guitar riff that Sam recognised after a moment as the Animals' 'House of the Rising Sun'. One of the men began singing along, substituting 'tide' for 'sun'. Sam wandered down the uncarpeted stairs, found Craig and a man she didn't recognise muttering quietly in a room that possessed a gas cooker, a large wooden table and a few chairs.

Craig glanced up at her. 'Jim's been arrested, we think,' he said. 'If you want to go, you can go now. We won't mention your involvement.'

Sam suddenly realised she liked Craig. He talked too much, and trusted too much – both bad for the leader of a subversive group, but nonetheless traits that Sam preferred to see in her friends.

'I'll stay in,' she said. 'Do we need to move on?'

'Jim won't talk,' said the other man. He had a London accent, and a heavy body, a big square head like a bull. He looked at Sam very directly for a moment. 'And who are you?'

Sam shrugged. 'I'm Sam Jones.'

'I'm Fred. Haystacks to my mates.' He patted his blond hair, square-cut. It did look like a haystack.

Sam knew she was talking to the group's real leader now. She wondered why he hadn't been at the festival or last night's action. Was he too well known?

'So why d'you want to be with us?' asked Haystacks.

'I think the System should change,' she said.

Haystacks raised an eyebrow.

Sam quickly added, 'I ran away from home when I was seventeen.' She blushed. 'With a man. We got separated…' She hesitated. 'Last summer. He went to America I think. Since then I've been roughing it with some folk in Hampshire.' Another pause, this time deliberate. She toed the floor, suddenly very aware of her nineties trainers. Would anyone notice the strange style, the brand that didn't exist? 'I'm bored. And I want to change things.'

'It takes more than being bored. You've got to have strength to make things change.'

Sam grinned. 'I've got strength.'

Haystacks rolled up a shirtsleeve, revealed a pale, hairy arm ridged with musculature. 'A lot of strength,' he said darkly.

Sam had to laugh. 'There's more than one way of being

strong.'

'There's only one way that works.'

Sam shook her head, then sat down at the table, rolled up her own sleeve. 'Wanna arm-wrestle, Haystacks?'

The man laughed. 'I don't think that would be fair!'

'Why not?'

The big man raised his eyebrows. 'I've never arm-wrestled with a girl before.'

'Well, there's always a first time,' said Sam. 'And try saying "woman". I'm more than sixteen.'

Haystacks glanced at Craig, who shook his head slowly. Then he pulled up a chair, sat down, and gripped Sam's proffered hand. Her arm seemed light, almost delicate, against his. But the muscles were there, and Sam knew it if the man didn't.

He pulled, not very hard. Sam flexed her back, brought as many muscles into play as she could. The movement caught Haystacks by surprise, and his arm crashed to the table. He looked surprised.

'You weren't trying!' she said, partly to cover his obvious embarrassment.

They started again. Pippa and Mike appeared at the doorway, watching. This time Haystacks used his full strength, and, even half rising from the chair and bearing down with all her weight, Sam found her arm dragged painfully to the table.

'Hey!' shouted Pippa. 'Don't hurt her!'

Sam ignored this. She met Haystacks' eyes. 'Best of three?'

He nodded, and they gripped hands again. His arm was hot against hers.

She closed her eyes, using one of the concentration

techniques that the Doctor had taught her. She revved her body with adrenalin, focused every muscle.

Haystacks pulled. She held him, pushed back, tipped their arms halfway to the table. His muscles began to shake: then, with a sudden twist, he slammed her arm across and hard on to the wood.

'Ow!' protested Sam, opening her eyes.

Haystacks smiled. 'You're very strong for a gir- for a *woman*,' he said. 'How do you do it?'

Sam said, 'Oh, it's a meditation technique the Doctor taught me. It increases your concentration, and your strength.'

'The Doctor?'

'The guy I was with. He calls himself that, because his real name's boring - John Smith.'

'Is that the same Smith that got you out of jail in Italy?' Pippa's voice. Sam could hear the suspicion there.

She glanced over her shoulder. 'Yes.' She shrugged. 'He's got connections.'

'What kind of connections?' asked Craig.

Sam looked down at the table, at her hand. She rubbed the bruised knuckles. 'Oh, hell.' One lie was as good as another. 'He's a viscount.'

'But he's on our side?' asked Haystacks.

Sam met his eyes. 'Oh, yes,' she said. 'He's on your side.'

'Then prove it. Get him to get Jimbo sprung from jail.'

Sam hesitated. 'I don't know whether he'd do that for me any more,' she said. 'But I can try. If I can contact him. If he's where I think he is.' That would leave her a way out if the Doctor couldn't or wouldn't help.

Haystacks nodded contemplatively. 'That's good enough,' he said. 'There's a phone outside.'

* * *

The first thing Fitz had felt was a roaring anger. The old lama, despite his name taken from the God of Chaos, had radiated a gentleness, an intense and quiet spirituality. It was his presence, not the few smuggled artefacts or the smiling young King George with his knife, that had made the old barn into a monastery. And the soldiers had shot the old man. Why? Retaliation? Intimidation? Because he'd refused to talk?

Gradually the anger had subsided, as the armoured car rolled and jolted its way along an increasingly rough and steep road. It had been replaced by a sickness, a deep sickness as Fitz's body was thrown against that of the dead man. He began to wonder what had happened to Maddie, whether she too was dead, in the back of the other car, or on the muddy village square. At the thought of that he was sick, a splattering of milky vomit over his trousers and the dead monk's robes.

After that, he banged at the metal walls of the car and yelled, until his throat was raw and his fists were bloody. No one took any notice.

He began to feel dizzy, and weak, and very, very cold. He was shivering violently when the car, at last, stopped.

Fitz waited, but the door didn't open. Metal clanged somewhere, there was some shouting. The air in the car got colder and colder.

Fitz banged on the metal again: at last, the shadow of a face appeared at the slit window.

'We will talk.' The English words were heavily accented.

But there was no talking, the face just vanished and the car started up again. Fitz hammered his fists against the metal, but there was no response. He stopped when he saw the blood dripping down his hands. 'Bugger,' he muttered.

The road was very steep now, the engine labouring. Fitz knew that they must be climbing into the mountains. He realised, with a growing panic, that the stop had probably been a border post, and that he was probably now in Tibet.

Chinese-occupied territory.

'You've got to let me go!' he shouted through the slot window. 'I'm a British citizen!'

There was no response. The light through the window was fading. Fitz realised that he was hungry, thirsty, and that if they didn't let him out soon he was going to soil his trousers.

He curled himself up against the side of the car furthest from the monk, and began to cry.

The phone dated from better days, perhaps the thirties: it was made from scratched, shiny, black Bakelite and had a faded brass dial. It looked discarded, on the bare floor in the hall, but there was a dialling tone.

The Doctor answered after three rings. Sam spoke as softly as she dared into the receiver, told him about the raid, and Jim's arrest.

'His full name's James Timothy Kelly. I don't know what the charges will be – criminal damage?'

A short silence at the other end. 'Where are you now?'

Speaking even more softly, Sam gave the address, adding, 'I think I might stay here for a while.'

'All right. I might pay you a visit.'

'Thanks.' Sam hung up, then heard a slight intake of breath behind her. She turned, saw Pippa staring at her. She hadn't changed, and there was a splash of red paint on her top.

'Why did you give our address?'

'He's a friend.' Sam shrugged. 'I trust him.'

'Well I don't. And I don't think you should be giving out this address to strangers.'

'I told you he's not a stranger!' snapped Sam. She was getting tired of Pippa's paranoia.

Pippa turned around and stormed upstairs. After a moment Sam heard her voice coming from one of the bedrooms.

Quietly, she followed, until she was close enough to hear the words.

'...friend... don't like... think...' The voice lowered to a whisper.

Sam crept closer, holding her breath. Pippa made the mistake of stressing her last words, and Sam could make them out.

'She might find the Revolution Man!'

'She won't know who he is.' Mike's voice. 'Don't worry so much.'

'Quiet!' hissed Pippa.

Sam quickly moved, making a noise on the stairs which she hoped would sound as if she were climbing them from the bottom. She almost ran into Pippa on the landing, had to meet her suspicious eyes.

But the young woman said nothing, just pushed past her and went down the stairs.

There was a knock at the front door.

Everything stopped, for a second. Then Sam became aware of a scrabbling noise – perhaps a mouse scrambling around behind the walls. A metallic clatter from downstairs.

The knock was repeated.

'Hello!' called a familiar voice. 'Is anybody home?'

The Doctor, she thought. I might have known.

She started down the stairs, saw Pippa standing by the

front door. 'It's OK,' said Sam. 'It's my friend. The Doctor.'

'So he was watching the house,' said Pippa simply. 'How else did he get here so quickly?' She opened the door.

Too late, Sam saw the long blade of the kitchen knife in Pippa's hand, saw it flash towards the Doctor's throat.

Chapter Twelve

Fitz dreamed, or half dreamed. Eastern harmonies and primary colours, a deep, sensuous beat, jasmine gardens, hash smoke and red buses, bowler hats and – *thud* – revolution – *bang*. A man in a green velvet jacket was shouting. '*You must find out, you must find* –' Then the voice stopped, echoing away to a silence.

Fitz realised how cold it was, and that he was awake. He was in the armoured car. In Tibet. A prisoner. He groaned at the realisation, and tried to sit up. He felt a cold, stiff object against his side.

The dead lama.

His guts heaved, but he managed not to be sick again. Outside, he could hear a faint, regular, mechanical sound. As it got louder, he recognised it.

A helicopter.

The noise became louder still, until Fitz was sure the machine was overhead, but it just continued to get louder and louder, until the entire car was shuddering, rocking from side to side.

Then the door was opened, and a draft of icy, diesel-smelling air rushed in. Fitz winced at a blaze of light, saw the silhouette of a soldier, felt hands grab him and manhandle him out of the car. His limbs jarred on stone, and he saw a steep slope of white snow fading away into darkness. He looked around for Maddie or King George, saw neither. A Chinese soldier was running with a pack, ducking in the fierce storm of grit coming from the helicopter. Fitz was

149

being dragged across the stone. Pain rivered up from his knee as it hit a projecting rock. Ice blew into his face.

If I'm going to escape, he thought, it has to be now.

But it was all he could do to stay conscious. The helicopter loomed, a mechanical dragon. Engines screamed. Fitz was thrown through a door into a darkened hold. He tried to stand, fell on to hard metal, as cold as ice. The door was slammed and the helicopter lurched into the air.

As his eyes adjusted, he saw that there were two soldiers standing guard over him, guns at their shoulders.

And again, next to him on the floor, a recumbent body.

This time it was King George. He was still alive: his eyes moved. But his face was bruised, his jacket bloodstained. Fitz reached out, only to discover that his hands had been roped behind his back. In the confusion, he hadn't even felt it happen.

'It is over,' whispered King George. 'Forgive me.'

'What's over?'

A painful echo of the broad smile. Fitz saw missing teeth, a split in the upper lip.

'I told them,' hissed the lama. 'I told them how to get to the valley of Om-Tsor.'

'Stop that!'

Haystacks had grabbed Pippa from behind and forced the knife out of her hand before Sam had reached the bottom of the stairs. The knife clattered on the ground; the Doctor picked it up, shrugged and took a step back while Haystacks dragged Pippa away from the door.

'Calm down!' snapped Haystacks, settling Pippa on the floor. 'This only makes things worse!'

'Violence usually does,' observed the Doctor, stepping inside cautiously. Sam saw a red welt across his throat from the knife. Had Pippa really intended to kill him?

She seemed calmer now, breathing deeply and staring at the Doctor, who was still holding the knife. Quietly, he passed it to Sam, who in turn passed it to Haystacks. The blond man rolled his eyes. 'Sometimes Pippa thinks everyone is the enemy,' he said, making an attempt at a smile, as if it had all been a big joke.

Sam decided this was the best way to play it. She cleared her throat and introduced everyone, keeping a wary eye on Pippa. Haystacks had an arm clamped around one of Pippa's, but that still left one arm free, which in her current mood might be one too many. Mike appeared in the background, holding a mug of tea. Craig clattered down the stairs, looked around.

'What happened?'

'Pippa had one of her paranoid moments again.' Haystacks was still keeping his voice casual. Pippa, released, went into the kitchen and began coughing.

The Doctor, rubbing his throat, said quietly, 'She's right to be paranoid. You've all got a great deal to worry about. But I'm not the problem.'

'Who is, then?' asked Craig.

'And who are you?' added Haystacks.

'It doesn't matter who I am. What does matter is knowing which one of you is the Revolution Man.'

There was a pause. A comical exchange of glances between the various anarchist comrades. A small shriek from Pippa in the kitchen.

Then Haystacks smiled. 'It's OK. He isn't any one of us. But he'll be here in a minute.'

Mike almost dropped his mug of tea, then frowned, and nodded. Sam glanced at the Doctor, wondering if he'd noticed the sequence of expressions, but he was looking at Haystacks.

Behind him, there was another knock on the door.

The Doctor opened it: and, for some reason, Sam wasn't entirely surprised to see the square-faced, compact form of Jean-Pierre Rex.

The helicopter had been travelling for an uncertain time, between minutes and hours. The air inside was freezing, and even the guards were shivering. King George lay still with his eyes closed. Only the occasional rise and fall of his chest showed that he was alive. Sometimes it stopped for so long that Fitz was sure the lama was dead, but then the blood-spattered surface of the leathers would heave again.

Suddenly he opened his eyes, looked at Fitz. 'We are nearly there,' he said, with a ghost of a smile.

Fitz frowned. 'Om-Tsor?'

King George whispered something, inaudible under the racket of the engine. Fitz felt hands on his shoulders, pulling him upright. He felt rough cloth scrape against the back of his neck, smelled sour flesh. Someone barked an order, and King George too was dragged to his feet. He was muttering something, perhaps a mantra.

Doors opened, revealing the cockpit of the craft. The controls and instruments looked primitive to Fitz: he realised he was still judging them against the technology of races hundreds, thousands, of years in the future. He had been with the Doctor only a few weeks, but it felt as if a huge chunk of his life, months, maybe years, had been spent in his company.

He wondered whether his bag had been taken from the village with him. Whether they'd searched it. Perhaps they'd found the card the Doctor had given him. Perhaps they'd even sent the signal. He glanced around the dark metal fuselage of the helicopter, almost expecting the TARDIS to appear.

A shove in the small of his back propelled him into the cockpit. King George was already there, making the small space behind the pilot's and copilot's seats cramped.

Below, through the windows, were mountains. Vast, pale, they rose like jagged ghosts into a mist-blue sky. As Fitz watched, the mist thinned, the light became brighter, and a pink-tinted light blossomed on the highest snow fields.

The pilot turned in his seat and barked at Fitz in Chinese. After a moment King George replied, pointing to the left. Fitz caught a glimpse of a valley of pale snow broken by jagged rocks, framed by ice. Then the helicopter lurched to one side, and Fitz almost fell over. Hands grabbed him, tried to pull him back. He resisted for a moment, then found himself falling back into the fuselage with one of the soldiers. If his hands had been free, he might have tried to fight; instead, the man rolled him over, kicked him in the ribs.

Fitz curled up in agony, his stomach roiling. He was unable to breathe, until at last his diaphragm unclenched and he took in a whooping breath.

Then more pain, and a mist in front of his eyes. Had the kick broken his ribs? He hadn't thought it possible for a simple kick to give so much pain.

The second kick sent him rolling across the icy metal floor. He tasted a bitter vomit in his mouth, and for a moment he had to concentrate on not choking. When he was able to draw breath again, more pain shot through his chest and belly.

When his vision cleared, he saw that the rear door of the chopper was open. A pale light was streaming in. At first he thought they'd landed, then he saw mountains drifting past the open door.

He was being picked up.

He was being picked up and carried towards the door.

They were going to throw him out.

He started to struggle, ignoring the pain in his chest. He tried to scream, but could only cough. He could see rocks below, pink-hinted snow, and a squat, brightly painted building, half covered in snow. His hand grasped metal for a moment – icy-cold metal – but his hold was broken. With another kick, he was falling.

He screamed this time, screamed despite the pain. He couldn't see the ground, could see only an icy blur, a dark shape, growing.

Then, he felt warmth. A warm wind, humid, like a southwesterly gale from the Atlantic.

My life must be flashing before my eyes, he thought. I didn't know it really happened like that.

But no scenes from his childhood appeared, thank Christ. Instead, he felt a gentle impact, as if he'd landed on a big warm cushion. He rolled, felt a solid surface, though he could still see the snow field below, the rocks getting closer.

But they were getting closer more and more slowly. When he was about ten feet up, he stopped. The snow dimpled, was pushed away, leaving a hollow space filled with small chunks of ice. He could see crumbled walls, a wooden gate. Something gripped his body, squeezing it. His chest gave a stab of pain, and he was lifted into the air. He could see the sky now, a deep morning blue. He couldn't breathe, and was beginning to feel dizzy. He felt an impact, and found himself lying in the doorway of the temple. The door was open, snow drifting across the floor inside.

He struggled into a sitting position, looked outside. The helicopter was coming in to land. It occurred to Fitz that whoever or whatever had rescued him had better do something about the chopper, or their efforts were likely to have been wasted.

Then it occurred to him to hide, just in case they didn't.

The engine note from the helicopter changed abruptly. Fitz saw it tilting, scudding away across the valley, then crashing to the ground, blades shattering. A second later the fuselage crumpled, like a crushed insect. Fuel exploded, two jets of orange flame, and black smoke rose.

The ground trembled. Fitz saw the snow field explode in several places across the valley, as if the place were being bombed. He looked inside the monastery, then it occurred to him that he would probably be safer in the open, if he could find shelter. He stood up, almost fell again, took a few tottering steps forward. Echoes of explosions were still rumbling around the valley, but there was no sign of any more bombs falling. He looked up at the sky, to see if there were any aircraft visible, but saw only the blue.

And a dark shape. Not a cloud.

A face. King George's face. And it was smiling.

'Goodbye, my friend.' It was a huge whisper, a murmur so loud that it shook Fitz's bones.

Then the face vanished, as if a light had been switched off.

Fitz retreated to the monastery doorway and sat down on

the polished stone there. Slowly, he worked it out: King
George must, somehow, have been carrying a small amount
of Om-Tsor. He'd taken it intending to destroy the helicopter,
but used it first to save Fitz's life. Then he'd died in the
wreck, with the Chinese soldiers he'd murdered.

Fitz couldn't help feeling grateful to King George, for the
warmth, for the safe landing. But it didn't alter the fact that
he was now stranded in an icy valley, probably a thousand
miles from anywhere, with no food and no water and no way
of getting out.

He wondered how long it would be before he joined King
George in nirvana, or wherever it was he'd gone. A day? An
hour?

He watched the sun rise, slow and bright, felt its weak
warmth on his face. He had begun shivering already, and his
legs were weak.

Without much hope, he turned and walked into the empty
monastery, where at least there was shelter.

They sat around the rough wooden table. A bottle of tomato
ketchup and another of milk stood in the middle. Mike and
Craig had mugs of coffee in front of them. Pippa was
drinking Coca-Cola, which Sam thought strangely ironic.

'So,' said Craig. He still hadn't slept – none of them had –
and there were shadows under his eyes. 'You're saying that
the action we held last night was no use at all?'

'Very little use.' Rex seemed distracted. He kept glancing at
the Doctor, as if they shared some deep secret. Yet the
possibility of his being the Revolution Man hadn't been
mentioned, and Sam seriously wondered if Haystacks had
been bluffing, or even just kidding. She didn't dare ask,

remembering how violently Rex had responded to the Doctor the previous year, and how he'd threatened her – perhaps got her arrested – in Rome.

'I have to agree with you about the action,' she said.

She noticed both Craig and Haystacks giving her surprised looks, but with Rex and the Doctor here her cover was blown anyway.

Rex nodded at her. 'And what would you propose as an alternative? What did you say last time we met – "peaceful means"?' His voice was thick with contempt.

'Effective use of minimum action,' said Sam.

'Like the arm-wrestling!' said Haystacks.

Everyone laughed, except the Doctor. He said, 'And what is *your* alternative, Jean-Pierre. Are you ready to tell me this time?'

Sam held her breath. Pippa gave a little gasp. Even Haystacks seemed surprised.

But Rex merely nodded. 'Why not?' He stood up. 'I am the Revolution Man. I'm proud of it. Arrest me if you want to.'

Chapter Thirteen

Fitz looked everywhere he could in the abandoned monastery, but there was nothing to eat, nothing to drink, no true shelter. There were endless passages of bare stone, high-ceilinged rooms with tiny windows, a great hall with carved-stone walls and a mud floor. Here and there coloured paint adhered to the walls, but most of the fixtures were gone. In fact, the place had a curiously incomplete air, for a supposedly centuries-old establishment: walls half built, arches with gaps in them. The stone was for the most part clean, fresh and unworn: this too seemed wrong for the centuries of age. In fact much of the building reminded Fitz of a film set.

Except, he thought grimly, that there was no producer here, no lighting crew, no one to call 'cut' and yell for the tea and sandwiches. There was only some limited shelter from the freezing wind, and drifts of snow forming strange patterns on the floor.

He found an intact flight of stairs, but, beyond a small stone gallery around the main hall, the first 'floor' had no floorboards nor any joists: just empty spaces above the spaces below. Again, Fitz was struck by the incompleteness of the building. He couldn't believe that the Chinese had destroyed the floorboards and the ceilings, as well as the fittings and furniture. And everything looked so new. Had King George been lying when he said the monastery was two centuries old?

Well, if there was no food or water or firewood here, then it wasn't going to matter.

He wondered how far it was to the nearest human settlement. If only he could get higher in the monastery – or higher up the valley – he might be able to see. It might even be possible to walk to somewhere.

He shivered. If he could just find some firewood, he would have a better chance of survival. But there were only the huge main doors, and he had no means of chopping them up, or of lighting the hard wood. If only he could find some Om-Tsor, he thought. Then, if what Maddie had said was true, he could walk away over the mountains. The trouble was, he would come back again when the trip ran out.

Then he remembered King George's story, how the lamas had kept the valley habitable using Om-Tsor to affect the climate. Perhaps he could do that – or, failing that, make himself an escape route.

It was worth a try.

First, of course, he had to find some Om-Tsor. King George must have had some – but there was no knowing how much, or whether any was left. Anyway, it probably wouldn't have survived the destruction of the helicopter. The wreck would probably still be hot from the fire – and when he thought about searching the bodies inside, Fitz decided against it. He even dismissed the idea of standing by the hot chopper for warmth. The thought of the smell of cooking human flesh made his stomach turn.

He wasn't that desperate yet. But hadn't King George said that the monastery had a garden, where Om-Tsor had been grown? Perhaps, despite the ice and freezing conditions, he might find some remnant there.

He climbed down the stairs to the floor of the hall, and was about to walk back to the main entrance when he realised something. The floor was mud, yes, but there were pathways in the mud, of broken stones, half covered by the frozen soil and drifted snow. If he imagined the pathways as they would have been before the snow had drifted in, the 'hall' looked increasingly as if it had been a garden. And what better place to grow the delicate plant than inside, sheltered from the winds?

He knelt down, wincing at the pain in his chest, and began scrabbling at the soil. It was frozen hard, like rock: he couldn't hope to shift it. He tried the snow instead, found that it would move, though it was compacted, more like solid ice than drifts. But there was no trace of any plants underneath, let alone anything that resembled the delicate butterfly-petal whiteness of Om-Tsor. He realised that it would be hard to see in the snow. His hands were getting numb, the flesh white under clumps of ice.

There had to be some way of finding Om-Tsor, here, in the place where it had all come from. He swore aloud, the curse echoing off the empty walls.

'You shouldn't use such language in the presence of an officer, mister!'

Fitz jumped up. The voice was heavily accented, in the singsong way of a Chinese or Hindi speaker. Fitz turned, ready to raise his hands in surrender. He saw a dark-skinned man, a round face, round pebble spectacles, surrounded by a thick hood and muffler.

'Don't know who I am?' The figure shuffled forward across the snow. Belatedly, Fitz realised that he was wearing an army-style greatcoat, with the dark-green cloth and red insignia of the Chinese People's Army. But he didn't seem to have a gun. 'I am Jin-Ming, to you. A friendly foe!' He began to

161

laugh, a long, self-congratulatory giggle, as if he'd just made the best joke in the world. He took several steps closer, until he was only three or four feet away, and stared at Fitz, without speaking, his expression seemingly puzzled.

'How did you get here?' asked Fitz.

More of the self-congratulatory giggling. 'You don't know? I'm in the Chinese Army, my man! We have ways and means, you know, ways and means!' He slapped his thigh and laughed some more, then sobered up and said, 'Tell me, what were you hoping to find here?'

Fitz took a breath. It occurred to him that just because the man was wearing an army greatcoat and said he was in the army didn't mean he was, in fact, a soldier. Perhaps he'd just found the greatcoat. Perhaps, even, at the site of the helicopter crash.

Fitz decided to play him at his own game. 'I could ask you the same thing.'

The man laughed hysterically. 'You could! You could indeed!' Suddenly there was a gun in his hand. A heavy, old-fashioned revolver. 'But, you see, you won't get an answer, because I've got the gun!' He fired it into the air. The shot echoed.

Fitz had barely had time to start panicking before he heard the sound of footsteps, running and shouts.

'See?' said Jin-Ming. 'My loyal troops.' He leaned closer, so that his breath was blowing into Fitz's face. It was hot, and smelled of something sweet and rotten. 'And you didn't believe I was an officer!'

'I don't –' began Fitz. Chinese soldiers poured in to the hall from two entrances.

'You were saying?' Jin-Ming was giggling again. He slapped

Fitz's arm. 'You were going to disagree?'

The soldiers were lining up in a way that Fitz found horribly reminiscent of a firing squad.

'What I would like to know,' said Jin-Ming conversationally, 'is what happened to our helicopter. I'm just curious. I mean to say, you'll probably tell me that your being here is just a coincidence, and then I'll have to take your word for that, as an officer. You are an officer, aren't you?'

If Jin-Ming thought he was an 'officer', then he thought he was a spy. Fitz stared at the brown face, the pebble glasses. The expression there was serious, but the face broke up into laughter again at the sight of Fitz's own puzzled and frightened face.

'Just a tourist, then? Got a bit lost? Just happened to have a ground-to-air missile on you?' He pushed Fitz's body, not hard, like a man making a joke in a pub. 'Amazing what tourists carry with them these days, don't you think?'

He looked over his shoulder and said something in Chinese. One of the men behind saluted, though Fitz detected a trace of confusion among the soldiers.

So Jin-Ming was a real Chinese officer, but he was mad: even his troops thought so.

Fitz felt his hands itching, looked down and saw only a few flakes of ice left. Water trickled down his fingers, sparkling in the light –

Wait. No. There was no light to make it sparkle.

And the remaining flakes weren't ice.

They were the shape of butterfly wings, and they were sparkling as they dissolved into the remaining drops of meltwater on his skin.

Om-Tsor.

Jin-Ming was already looking at Fitz's hands, having followed his glance.

'Ah! You have been digging in the ice, I see. Funny that! That's just what we were planning to do! Have you found anything, I wonder?'

He doesn't know what he's looking for, thought Fitz. At least, he doesn't know what it looks like.

Quickly, before he could think, before Jin-Ming could think, he put his hands to his mouth and crammed the flakes of Om-Tsor inside.

For a couple of seconds, nothing happened, except that a puzzled expression formed on Jin-Ming's face.

'Now why did you do that?' he asked.

Fitz didn't know. All he could see were colours, numbers, lights.

Then he was standing above the world, the mountains like frozen waves below him. The sky was black. He couldn't see the monastery, but he could see India, the whole sharp green-brown plain, the curl of the Ganges and the Brahmaputra.

It took him a second to realise what had happened. Then it hit him: he'd taken too much of the stuff, or taken it in the wrong way, or –

Something had gone wrong, anyway.

He was about fifty miles high.

'It wasn't entirely under my control,' admitted Rex. 'I found myself doing things I hadn't intended. That's why I stopped.'

His face was curiously bright, the round glasses catching the sun. They were sitting on an old bench in the garden of the Total Liberation Brigade's house. The place was overgrown with flowers, which looked as if they hadn't been tended in a while. There was a fish pond, watched by a lazy black cat. Sam wondered if there were any fish.

'You stopped?' The Doctor was standing, balanced on a duckboard that crossed part of the pond, his eyes focused on the blue sky.

'Yes. After the Rome embassy. When I drew the sign there, two people died. They were employees of a corrupt system, of a system that destroyed lives. But they were people. Young women. Quite beautiful, and one a mother of two children. I started this because I didn't want people to die. Now I was doing the killing myself. I stopped.'

The Doctor nodded distantly. He clearly wasn't in the mood for giving human sympathy at the moment. Sam said quickly, 'You did the right thing, Jean-Pierre.'

'We need to know which incidents you were responsible for,' said the Doctor. 'A complete list. You won't be prosecuted.' He stepped off the duckboard, adjusted the collar of his jacket. 'And we need to know where you were getting the Om-Tsor, too.'

'I can't tell you that.'

The Doctor leaned down in front of the bench, so that his face was level with Rex's and cast a shadow over it. 'Whoever's using Om-Tsor now is killing more people,' he said fiercely. 'And the substance is a danger to the entire planet. I need to know where it is so that I can stop it being used any more. Before it's too late for all of you.'

'I can't tell you,' repeated Rex. 'I don't even know whether my contact is still alive.'

'Yes you do,' said the Doctor. 'Because you're still using Om-Tsor.'

Rex's face flushed with angry red blood, and for a moment Sam thought they'd lost him, that he would walk out as he had the last time. But then he nodded. 'It's true. I still use it. I have to: it is habit-forming. But I no longer touch the world. I just walk above it, and watch.' He stood, looked down into the murky pond. Sam thought she saw a glint of gold. 'I never knew how beautiful it was.' He shrugged.

'And where do you get Om-Tsor?' The Doctor's question was gentle, at last. In fact his entire manner had changed, as if there were some subtext to Rex's statements. Sam frowned, decided she would ask him about it afterwards.

Rex was still staring at the pond. 'One fish, two fish, three fish, four. Why not tell you? But you might have to be careful.'

'We know that,' said the Doctor and Sam, simultaneously. They looked at each other. The Doctor grinned.

Rex shrugged again. 'I get it here. This house. That is why I am here this morning.'

Sam and the Doctor looked at each other again. She was sure that they were both wondering why they hadn't thought of it hours ago.

They set off at a run for the house.

It was empty, apart from a mug of cold coffee and a spilled bottle of tomato ketchup on the wooden kitchen table.

It took Fitz about a minute to work out that he didn't need to breathe, that his real body was still breathing, that he didn't need to panic.

By then, he was all but in orbit, and he could see a smudged footprint in the Himalayas, about five miles long, with ragged curtains of snow settling around its edges. He remembered Maddie, the falling train. Wondered about earthquakes. About

Chinese soldiers, scurrying to pick up Om-Tsor around his real body. A battalion of fifty-mile-high giants, with a mission to destroy the capitalist world.

It didn't sound good.

I need to get back to the lamasery, he thought. And I need to get back fast. Before Jin-Ming works out what's happened, that I haven't just fainted or poisoned myself. Then he'll probably shoot me.

He tried to orientate himself, but it was difficult. He was over the coast now, a ragged muddle of brown and green islands breaking into a polished blue sea. Clouds like white seeds floated against the green land. Fitz could feel jungles, smell rain.

I need to be smaller, he thought. Smaller and back in the mountains.

He could see the Himalayas: they looked like white water, a choppy sea rearing from the plain green of the jungle. He tried to swim through the air towards them, but his hands were clumsy and he could feel no air resistance. He realised that he was probably above most of the atmosphere. And if he walked on the ground... He looked at the crowded plains below him and shuddered.

No wonder the Doctor had said that this stuff could mean the end of the world.

Fitz tried to will himself towards the mountains, was rewarded by a feel of ice, a taste of cold air, and a jerky movement to a world of icecaps and purple horizons. Space was still black above.

Now where the hell was the valley?

There was a disturbance in front of him. For a moment, Fitz thought the moon was rising. Then he saw the dark brown features of Jin-Ming, the bright pebble glasses, the muffler, the army greatcoat.

The man giggled. 'Hello, my friend!' he boomed. 'It seems we are bigger than we thought!' He looked down at the snow fields, raised his eyebrows. 'Wonderful!' He looked up again, then extended his arms, fists clenched. 'Winner takes the Earth, loser gets the moon? How's that, eh?'

Chapter Fourteen

Maddie knew she was going to die. The carriage was creaking as it fell, like a rocking chair moving on an old wooden floor. It twisted, and the cliffs outside the moving windows were endless, like a waterfall of grey rock. Hundreds of monkeys were watching her, clinging to the inverted seats, squatting on the roof that had become the floor. Their mouths were gaping in screams, and black blood was streaming from their eyes…

Maddie opened her eyes, gasping, saw a dark timber roof, and a smoky haze which slowly dissolved. Her face, her entire body, felt flushed – almost on fire. The dream still danced in front of her eyes, and eyes were still watching her.

She rubbed her eyes, focused, and saw that the eyes belonged to a child. His small face and bright eyes did make him look like a monkey, and there was something monkey-like in his movements as he sprang to his feet, jumped and shrieked, bounded away towards the light. Maddie heard footsteps, saw leather-clad legs approaching, ending in bare feet – old, curled, clawlike. She tried to sit up, but the effort was too much. She saw wooden walls, mud and straw on bare boards. A shrivelled face looked down on her, and spat. A voice gabbled, a long slur of syllables that made no sense.

Nepali. Nepal. She was in Nepal, and Fitz –

Fitz had been taken away. She remembered that, remembered that he'd been dragged through the door of the barn-monastery, but remembered nothing else.

She struggled to sit up again, felt a sharp pain in her belly, as if she had been stabbed. Her eyes watered, and she heard herself gasping for breath. She saw the dry blood staining her coat, and decided it was real. She clenched her fists against the pain, closed her eyes.

When she opened them, she saw two dun-coloured objects resting against the wall.

Backpacks. Hers and Fitz's. She thought about antibiotics, bandages. Gestured towards the packs.

Fitz –

'My friend,' she said. 'What happened to my friend?'

More incomprehensible syllables. But the old woman was shuffling towards the packs. She lifted one of them – Fitz's – brought it over, fiddled with the straps. At last she got it open.

Maddie was too weak to get anything out of the pack. She tried, but it was as if her hands were scrabbling around the furry body of an animal. Everything felt warm, soft. Things moved, but nothing would come out of the pack. She began to feel dizzy and faint.

The old woman pushed her back gently, began removing clothes from the pack, and a sandwich box (did that have the bandages?), house shoes (why had Fitz taken those?). More cloth – a scarf? Maddie lay back, winced at another stabbing pain from her belly. Perhaps it would be better just to rest. She was terribly thirsty. She crudely mimed drinking, and the old woman nodded, walked away.

Maddie wondered if she'd been shot. Again. She didn't dare look, didn't dare touch the cloth wrapped around her stomach. She rummaged around in the pack again, in case the woman had missed something. But why would that help?

She found herself stroking a crude seam at the bottom of

the pack, picking at loose strands of cotton.

The card. The Doctor. Call the Doctor.

It won't work, Fitz, she thought. I don't know who he is and I don't know where you are.

The old woman was returning with a wooden bowl. Wisps of steam rose from the bowl, curling around the handle of a wooden spoon. For a moment, Maddie was bizarrely reminded of the moment in Ed's attic with the teacups full of Om-Tsor, the vapour rising.

A spoonful of steaming soup was put in front of her nose, but Maddie only felt sick. She tried to sip at the liquid, felt her stomach heave. A wave of pain and dizziness came over her.

Call the Doctor.

Her hand was still inside the pack, touching the crude seam where Fitz must have stitched an extra pocket into the material. She pulled at it, gestured at the woman. The wizened face frowned. Maddie noticed that the woman had pigtails, like a little girl, but grey and wispy white.

'Please…' she said. 'Inside. There's something sewn into the lining.'

The woman probably hadn't understood the words, but she took the bag and pulled at the lining for a moment, then walked away, to return with a knife. She cut open the material, pulled out a dark plastic card whose surface flashed in the light. She frowned at it, then handed it to Maddie.

Maddie studied the card. It was dark blue, with white writing: PUBLIC CALL BOX, it said. PRESS TO CALL. There was a raised button, like a small, white, hatched window.

Maddie pressed the button.

For a few seconds nothing happened. She was just about to press it again when the building started to tremble. The soup bowl, which the old woman had left on the floor, began to slop its contents as the floor rocked to and fro like a boat in a storm. Small pieces of dry thatch began to fall from the ceiling.

The woman was staring at Maddie, her face twisted into an almost caricature expression of fear.

'Bai-lal!' she shrieked. 'Bai-lal!'

Maddie wanted to explain, wanted to tell the woman that it wasn't magic, but she wasn't sure she believed that, or even whether that was what the other was saying.

But there was no time to speak, or explain anything, because a crack was opening up in the wall behind her, letting in the daylight.

From above, pieces of the roof began to fall.

'Right,' said the Doctor. 'You take the upstairs, I'll take the downstairs.'

Sam nodded, though she didn't see the point. The Total Liberation Brigade would undoubtedly have liberated themselves via the front door. It was possible they'd left the Om-Tsor behind, but not very likely.

Upstairs were four bedrooms, each smelling mustier than the last, each with a rumpled double bed or a pair of singles. There was one wooden wardrobe, daubed with psychedelic purples and yellows, and a few low vinyl tables stacked with books and records: apart from that, the TLB didn't seem to believe in furniture. There was certainly no trace of anything that resembled Om-Tsor as the Doctor and Fitz had described it. But ten years' supply could have been concealed in a shoebox under the floorboards.

From downstairs there was a high-pitched warbling. It

sounded very out of place in sixties' suburbia, and Sam wasn't surprised when she heard the Doctor's shout, 'Sam – I'm going to be needed somewhere else five minutes ago.'

She yelled an acknowledgement, heard the front door slam.

'OK, so I'll take the downstairs too,' she muttered. 'No problem. And don't tell me where you're going. That would make it too easy.'

She went downstairs, stopped in the hall. The fat black cat was flat against the floor, his limbs spread, his tail straight out behind. He looked like a cartoon cat squashed by a ton weight, and for an instant Sam thought he was dead. Then she saw his eyes open and stare at her before, with a clatter of claws, he scrambled past her and up the stairs.

What had scared him? The Doctor's paging device? Or something more serious?

She saw the garden door open, and walked out.

She stopped.

Jean-Pierre Rex's head was floating in the fish pond. Just the head – the skin of the face blue, the eyes distended with terror. The rest of the body had vanished, but a trail of blood led over the fence at the back of the garden.

Sam hesitated, just too long.

Pond water slurped, stirred, sprayed across the garden. Something knocked her over, pressed down on her body. She half got up, felt her chest squeezed as if between two giant fingers, though she could see nothing except a few strands of pond weed hanging in the air. It was like a dream, a nightmare of strangulation. She could see the house door, still open, the bright flowers, the hot June sun.

She could feel the breath being squeezed out of her body.

'Doctor!' she tried to shout. 'Help!'

But she knew that the Doctor was gone.

Fitz made it to the Indian Ocean before Jin-Ming caught up with him. He'd got away by jumping, using the ankle-high mountains as launching pads. He'd half expected to feel the crushing pain as the monastery collapsed over his real body, but nothing had happened. Instead he was somersaulting out across the blue ocean, far above the world.

Jin-Ming caught him in a rugby tackle, and they both fell towards the sea. Fitz imagined what the impact of two fifty-mile-high giants would do to the ocean, and kicked out at Jin-Ming's face. It worked: the man grunted, let go. But Fitz discovered he had one knee on the rough stone, water soaking his trouser leg. Waves that must be the size of small mountains rolled with a horrible, true-to-life slowness across the blue.

The moon, he thought. We should fight on the moon. There aren't any people there.

He imagined himself flying – *was* flying as he mentally pushed the Earth back.

A huge weight landed in his belly, and he saw Jin-Ming, a monstrous size now (how did you control the size?), and a boot in his stomach.

He was falling. He stopped the fall by willing it, but not before he had reached a layer of cloud. As he floated up again, he could see a man-shaped gap in the cloud, could see the quick vortices filling the hole, the blue-grey tails of tornadoes around the edge. There was land below: India?

Didn't Jin-Ming care how much damage they did?

He was still there, in space, his body starkly half lit, like a strangely shaped moon. He seemed to be smaller again.

With an effort of will, Fitz made himself bigger. It wasn't difficult. The Earth seemed to shrink.

Jin-Ming watched, gave a tinny giggle. 'Be careful! You might hurt someone!' He slapped his thigh, somersaulted towards the Earth and vanished.

A moment later, the Earth vanished too, and Fitz found himself looking at the barrel of a gun, held by a stern-faced Chinese soldier.

He looked around, saw Jin-Ming lying in an undignified heap, the other soldiers sweeping ice into large sacks.

After about a minute, Jin-Ming's eyes opened, and met Fitz's.

'Well, that's Washington taken care of. Flat as a pancake!' He giggled. 'It's always so good to do some useful work, don't you think? Useful work!' He appeared to find the idea hysterically funny. 'Now, my brother officer –' more giggles – 'how about Beijing, and some political education? Or would you prefer to be shot? I leave it up to you!'

Laughing, he staggered towards the door. The soldiers saluted him, one by one.

'Did you really attack Washington?' Fitz called after him, hoping it was only Jin-Ming's mad sense of humour. 'You could have started World War Three!'

More hysterical laughter was the only reply.

Maddie didn't know that she knew the sound until she heard it, above the wailing of the old woman and the screams of children, above the howling of the wind through the cracked walls of the hut.

A deeper, more regular howling. The sound of a wind

blowing through space and time, perhaps. She'd heard it once before, in the hospital, and had known it for a sort of magic then. Now, despite Fitz's assurances about the card, it seemed like a miracle.

She watched the blue box slowly materialise against the far wall, wondered about miracles. When the door opened, she almost recognised the man who emerged.

He picked his way through the dust of the floor, stepped over the broken soup bowl, bent down to look at her.

'Fitz is gone,' she managed to say. 'At least I think he is. The Chinese took him. He might be dead.'

The Doctor looked down at her with an expression of great compassion – so much so that Maddie wondered if she too was going to die. She was rather surprised when he merely leaned down and helped her to stand. His hands were warm. Her stomach hurt, but not nearly as much as she had expected it to.

'Don't worry about Fitz,' he said, smiling. 'He can take care of himself, I expect.' He put on a slightly flustered expression, like a favourite uncle who's forgotten your Christmas present. He was a little too young for that face, but Maddie found it immensely reassuring nonetheless. She let him lead her into the blue box, stared in confusion at the huge space, cluttered with objects. There was even a car parked inside. Had it been this big before?

Then the Doctor screamed.

For a moment, Maddie thought it was a scream of pain. She jumped back, tensing against whatever it was that was attacking him. Then she saw that there was no attacker: he was tearing at his hair, staring at one of the television-like screens above a console thing in the centre of the room. And his scream wasn't totally incoherent: she could make out words.

'Oh, no! Sam Sam *Sam*! How could I have been so *stupid*?'

He hit switches on the console, and the central column began to move. A groaning, whistling sound filled the room. Maddie took a deep breath, told herself not to be afraid. Fitz had said it was weird, and it was – but he'd also returned unhurt from several journeys.

She walked across the floor, touched the Doctor on the arm. 'Do you need any help?'

The Doctor glanced at her. 'Keep an eye on the date counter, Maddie. Make sure it doesn't move.' He tapped a brass calendar with black and white figures on it that said '5 June 1968 HUMANIAN ERA'. Maddie wondered how many eras there were, how long they were. How little the others had to do with the life of humans.

The floor of the room began to move underneath her. It wasn't the steady motion of a ship at sea, more the irregular lurch of a rowing boat as you step aboard: Maddie almost lost her footing. A stab of pain from her stomach made her wince.

She looked at the figures. They hadn't changed.

Abruptly, the motion of the strange vehicle stopped. A single, gonglike alarm rang out. Unsteady currents of air ran about the huge space, like stray winds before a storm. Then the doors opened, and a body tumbled in, whirling loose like a rag doll. It was a moment before Maddie decided that it must a real person, that the blue colour of the face was caused by asphyxia and not a dye.

The Doctor was shouting, 'Sam! Sam! Sam!' He ran to the young woman's side, began pounding at her chest with his hands.

She gave a single, whooping breath. The Doctor let go,

waited. 'Come on, Sam!'

The woman breathed again, and again; slowly, colour returned to her cheeks, and her eyes opened. Amazingly, she smiled. 'You left that one a bit late, Doctor.' Her voice was thick, low.

'You're alive!' yelled the Doctor. He got up and did a little dance. 'You're alive! You're alive!'

The woman – Sam – got up and smiled, then coughed and winced. She glanced at Maddie. 'Hello. You're Maddie, aren't you? Are you all right?'

Maddie shrugged. 'Not really.' She hesitated, then added, 'And you?'

Sam stood up, winced again. 'I'll survive.'

'Do you know what's happened to Fitz?' asked Maddie.

Sam shook her head. 'I think we all need a rest. Then we can talk.'

But the Doctor said, 'I don't think there's time for that.' Behind his voice, the gong sound was booming out, again and again and again.

Sam was at the Doctor's side. She didn't say anything, or ask anything: it was obvious that she and the Doctor had worked together for a long time, and didn't always need words.

Maddie's legs started to shake, and she realised how tired she was. She sat down on the floor, closed her eyes.

She felt a hand on her arm, opened her eyes and saw Sam sitting down with her. Her expression was serious.

'What is it?'

'The TARDIS... um, this ship, it's detected another Om-Tsor event – someone using the drug. It's got a lot worse – whatever we've done has made things worse.'

Maddie swallowed. She couldn't understand. Could the

178

Doctor see into the future? 'Worse than what?' she asked.

'Worse than everything,' said the Doctor solemnly. 'On the eighteenth of May, nineteen sixty-nine, the Earth will cease to exist.'

Maddie felt a surge of panic. This couldn't be happening. She stood up, saw at the calendar on the console.

It read '2 January 1969', and as she watched the figures were wheeling forward.

Press Reports 1968-9

Times of India, 1 July 1968:

Following the extraordinary storms and tidal waves last month which tragically cost so many lives, the Indian government has accused China of a deliberate attack on Indian sovereign territory and of terrorising the population.

So far the Chinese Government has made no excuse or indeed any reply, but nonetheless the Indian Army has been mobilised in the provinces of Assam and Bengal, as a precaution against any repeat of the invasion of 1961.

The Government of Pakistan has said that it regards the mobilisation as a hostile act, particularly in the light of the damage done to East Pakistan by the tidal waves. Pakistan has mobilised its forces in the area, and is even claiming that the damage was caused by the Indian Government 'working mistakenly on a secret weapon'.

The Times, 12 November 1968:

Events in the Vietnam War took a startling turn yesterday when the so-called 'Revolution Man' took the side of the North Vietnamese.

The US aircraft carrier *Constitution*, stationed in the Gulf of Tongking, has been incapacitated. The Pentagon will not release details, but it is rumoured that the deck of the carrier has been torn up, and the famous capital R symbol of the Revolution Man has been carved across the broken metal.

The Pentagon has, however, confirmed that 14 US servicemen lost their lives in the attack on the carrier.

According to weapons experts at the Ministry of Defence in London, it is quite inconceivable that any weapon currently known to either the Americans or the Soviet Union could generate a field of the kind needed to disrupt matter in the way that the 'Revolution Man' is able to do. The fact that the weapon has been used against both countries seems to strengthen suspicions that another country – possibly China – may be involved.

Washington Post, 4 January 1969:

US Defense Forces went to Def Con 2 last night – the highest state of alert short of outright war – following an attack on a US Air Force base in High Raccoon, Tennessee. The symbol of the mysterious 'Revolution Man' was carved across the blacktop, incapacitating the base and its force of B-52 bombers.

Since the bombers are part of the US strategic nuclear deterrent, the President was alerted at once and gave the instruction to prepare for war. It is understood that President Johnson used the 'hotline' to call Soviet Premier Leonid Brezhnev. The Soviet leader apparently told Mr Johnson that the Russians had no knowledge of the attack and no weapon that could have carried it out.

Nonetheless it is the opinion of the Defense Department that we can take no chances. In a grim briefing this morning, the Defense Secretary told reporters – and the world – that the US would not tolerate further attacks on its strategic nuclear forces 'by the so-called Revolution Man or by anybody else'. Further attacks, he said, might lead to a global thermonuclear conflict 'from which no one could possibly emerge as the victor'. He pleaded with whoever or whatever is responsible for these attacks to cease their activities 'so that the world can return to a state of calm and peace, before it is too late.'

Book Three
1969

Chapter Fifteen

The mission would begin today.

Fitz knew it even before he woke up, knew it from the sharp feel of the stiff sheet against his skin. In his dreams, there had been kaleidoscopes of blue and copper, forming and reforming crystals of pure, distilled, time.

When he did wake, Fitz didn't sit up. Not at first. It would be too early: he would disturb the others. So he just opened his eyes and stared at the grey ceiling. The crystals still seemed to dance there, faintly. 'There was a young lady called Bright,' he muttered, 'Who travelled much faster than light…'

Which might be how the Doctor did it.

No. Forget the Doctor. The Doctor was an individualist, essentially an entrepreneur. His methods couldn't possibly succeed.

Fitz got out of bed, as quietly as he could, and placed his bare feet on the rough matting. No one stirred in any of the other bunks. A fly buzzed around the room, its body ticking against the green netting that covered the windows. At the end of the room, above the door to the canteen, Mao's portrait stared down from the wall. His clothes were blue-grey and severe, his expression distant. Underneath was the name of the collective, in neatly stencilled Chinese characters: Chairman Mao Ideal Collective. Fitz stared at the portrait for a moment, then walked outside.

It was hot: the fields were stark, tall green blades surrounded by grey soil. Mountains rose sheerly behind them, mossed with small trees. The sky was blue and the sun was brass. Fitz realised that he was happy. He didn't know for certain when he'd started to be happy, when the pain had gone, but he knew for certain that he was happy now. His life made sense at last, here under the blue brass hot sky of Sichuan. In the past, if anyone had talked to him about making the perfect life, building a better world, he had sneered at them, his innate cynicism telling him that it must be impossible. He supposed, deep down, he'd never believed the Doctor and his talk of a future for the human race: how could such a bunch of dangerous failures have a future?

But now he could see that future, see the world from which all the splinters of possibility had diverged. It was here in front of him, the ordered fields, the farmers who worked hard, for a fair return. He could hear the scythes out in Glorious Victory field now, where they were harvesting hay. The regular crackle of the grass breaking formed a rhythm like a slow clock, a clock at the centre of time.

The Doctor was wrong, thought Fitz. He meant well, with his individual problem fixing, his life saving, his flea-hops around the framework of the universe. But in the end, only a coherent vision could save lives, and make those lives worth living. Fitz knew now that he'd been looking for that vision with the Doctor, and again when he had left: he thought he'd found it in love, with Maddie. But bourgeois "love" offered no permanent solution either: it just hid the problem in a cloud of sexual pleasure. There was only one solution, one vision, that would save humanity in the long run. A vision that gave everyone a fair return for their labour. A vision that allowed the slow tick of the scythe to govern the world. A vision of peace.

The vision of Chairman Mao.

Fitz heard footsteps behind him, turned and saw his friend and colleague Jin-Ming. The brown, sunny face was cracked in a smile as usual, the teeth yellow as nuggets.

'I see you are wool-gathering, my friend. Remember what our Chairman says about that!'

Fitz swallowed. For an instant, pain, thirst and darkness flickered in front of his vision. There was something about Jin-Ming...

Who could be trusted as a follower of Mao. Who was trusted by Mao.

Fitz met the older man's eyes. 'I was just thinking that it's a shame that I'm leaving.'

'The mission is necessary,' said Jin-Ming quietly. 'It must be necessary, eh? Or it wouldn't be a mission!'

'Yes, of course.' Sometimes Jin-Ming's insistent sense of humour got on Fitz's nerves.

The other man seemed to sense this, because he instantly became more serious. 'You know what the position is with the Om-Tsor drug. The quantities we found in Tibet were insufficient, and all our attempts at growing it from seed have failed. But we need that drug, if the People's Republic is to survive at all.'

Fitz nodded. But he felt a niggling doubt, like a corner of darkness on a bright field. Jin-Ming seemed to sense it: his brown face creased, and he said, 'Is there any problem, Comrade? Any last minute assistance that you need?'

'Can we trust these Anarchists - this Total Liberation Brigade?' he asked Fitz at last, 'If they aren't part of our

Revolution, they'll want something in return. What are we giving them?' Asking the question made him feel guilty and confused: he was using alien thought processes, as he had in his former life.

Jin-Ming looked away, at the low grey buildings of the main compound. There was a long silence. Something rustled in the long maize: perhaps a bird. Fitz wondered whether he should shout, to disturb the raider. But Jin-Ming grabbed his arm, said quietly, 'There is something we will give them, and you will help with that too. Come on, it's time to go.'

He led Fitz around the main compound, through the vegetable gardens, where the huge cabbages and tomato plants were still shadowed and silver with dew. Then they walked down to the small wooden guardhouse at the main gate, where two soldiers of the People's Army were stationed to keep capitalist sympathisers and spies from disrupting the life of the Ideal Collective.

The soldiers saluted Jin-Ming, and raised the barrier to let them pass. Once outside, they walked a little way down the road, between tall fences and even taller young pines, until they came to an olive-coloured Army truck with an open back. Two young men in uniform lounged in the back, shouldering long guns. When they saw Jin-Ming they jumped out of the truck and saluted.

Vaguely discomfited, Fitz jumped up on to the back of the truck. Jin-Ming joined him, the motor started, and they were on their way.

The young men with the guns were watchful, watching the road, watching Fitz. He began to feel there was something wrong, but he couldn't say what it was.

* * *

The console room floor jolted as if something had hit it, and Sam realised that the TARDIS had landed – or at least, stopped careering forward through time.

The Doctor glanced at her from the console. 'Just in time!'

'The fourteenth of February,' reported Maddie, who was standing by the calendar read-out. Sam noticed that her long red hair reached almost to her waist.

'It's St Valentine's day!' said the Doctor.

For a moment Sam was flummoxed, then she remembered the custom: exchanging cards, lovers' vows, hugs and kisses, candlelit dinners.

She sighed. Life had too many other things in it, right now, for all that. Perhaps if she and the Doctor could ever settle down… She grinned at the thought. 'Hi. I'm Sam, and this is my friend the Doctor. We save the Universe six times before breakfast each morning, and we live in an intradimensional Police Box that might take off for Sigma Draconis at any moment. How do you feel about starting a relationship with me?'

Maybe not.

Anyway, the world was supposed to end in about three months unless she and the Doctor got off their backsides and did something about it. She walked over to Maddie, who was looking a bit shell-shocked – her face was white, and she was clinging to the console as if the TARDIS were still rocking like a ship at sea. It was hardly a surprise in the circumstances.

The Doctor was still fussing around, prodding at switches, examining read-outs and screens. Sam said firmly, 'I don't care if the world's going to end next Tuesday. Maddie and I need some rest. And don't tell me there isn't time, because there's going to have to be. We're certain to have a lot to do and we need to be alert to do it.' She didn't add *I was nearly killed about five minutes ago and my chest hurts and I feel like fainting*, because she knew she didn't need to.

The Doctor looked up with a puzzled expression, then smiled faintly. 'Oh! Sleep! Of course! I suppose it is a necessity sometimes, yes...' He frowned in the direction of the TARDIS library, the ranks of books and pseudo-books that lined one wall of the console room, the door that led to a million more. 'In any case, I need to do some research – I think.'

'I want to find Fitz,' said Maddie suddenly. 'I feel I got him into this.'

'Fitz?' Sam was startled, but when she thought about it... He had left the TARDIS because of Maddie. Why shouldn't he still be with her?

She asked Maddie what had happened, and received a brief account of the expedition to Tibet. The Doctor looked on, didn't say a word.

Sam thought about it. The Chinese soldiers could have taken Fitz anywhere. Presumably they'd tried to find the valley of Om-Tsor. After that... She turned to the Doctor. 'Is there any way we can search –'

He interrupted her question by shaking his head. 'Sorry, Sam. Can't be done, or I'd be doing it now. Tibet is huge, China is even bigger. We've no idea where Fitz is, and no way of tracing him without the card, which was left with –' He nodded at Maddie.

'I wasn't asking you to find him,' said Maddie. 'I'll look myself, if you'll take me there.'

'Maddie, Maddie, Maddie. Didn't you hear me? China is big. Big, big, big, big, hu-u-uge. Half a continent. And it's in a state of chaos, being ruled over by an old dictator with more egoism than sense.' A pause. 'Of course, I suppose I could ask him to –' He shook his head. 'He'd never believe me. Not now. He got paranoid in his old age.'

'Who?' asked Maddie, obviously confused.

'Mao. Shame, really. He started out with some good ideas. But he just couldn't see that people aren't simple machines, and don't follow simple rules. Reward and punishment aren't buttons on a dashboard. It's like the TARDIS. It's not the switches, its how and when you press them. And people are infinitely more complicated.' He smiled at Sam. 'I think that's why I like them.'

Sam just smiled back, but Maddie said, 'You know *Mao*?'

The Doctor shrugged. 'Knew. In a previous – well, a long time ago. When he was still… Before he lost… oh, well, I've been through that.' He looked up at the screens. 'Look, I'll keep an eye on things here. Both of you should get some rest. Unless you want to go now, Maddie.'

Maddie shook her head. 'I'll stay. I'm not sure if I'll sleep, though. This place freaks me out.'

Sam glanced at her, not altogether surprised. There had been many people – human and alien – who'd seen the inside of the TARDIS in the time she'd been with the Doctor. Not many had liked it, or wanted to stay. In some ways, she'd been surprised that Fitz had stayed as long as he had.

Sam took her arm. 'You can have my room,' she said. 'There's a folding bed.' She'd bought it in case she ever had visitors: it was a 23rd Century model, adjustable for all sizes of human and several types of humanoid alien. She'd never used it: she only hoped she didn't press the button for a Draconian or an Earth Reptile by mistake.

As Sam led the way through the maze of TARDIS passageways with their bizarre mixture of styles and fittings, Maddie's expression became increasingly wary. 'I don't think I'll be able to find my way out,' she complained.

'I sometimes have trouble with that,' admitted Sam. She smiled sidelong at Maddie. Some of the colour had returned to the younger woman's face, but Sam still wasn't sure whether she shouldn't check to see whether she was seriously hurt.

'How well did you know Fitz?' asked Maddie suddenly.

Sam hesitated, met the woman's eyes. 'Not that well,' she said with a slight smile. 'Why?'

Maddie blushed. 'Oh, I just wondered.'

'I don't want him to come to any harm,' said Sam.

'Of course you don't,' said Maddie. 'It's just that – when you've cared for someone – I mean, when you've done *that* with them –'

Sam waited. The TARDIS hummed around them.

'You just feel differently. I have to go back. Try and find him. I mean, this – TARDIS, it can go back in time, can't it?'

Sam nodded. 'But before you say it, no, we can't change what's already happened. We were involved in a paradox loop once before, and we almost didn't get out.' She hoped her tone of voice was convincing.

Maddie looked down. Sam realised that the younger woman's face was dirty, and that she was on the verge of tears.

She put an arm round her shoulders. 'Look – we're both tired out. Why don't we talk about this in the morning?'

Maddie shrugged. 'OK.'

They walked to Sam's room. She found the bed, unravelled it, set it to what she hoped was the correct size of human. Then she took a look at Maddie's stomach, and found a messy, shallow wound on the verge of becoming infected: she bandaged it with an antigenic gauze. Maddie was almost asleep before Sam had finished with the bandage.

Sam pulled off her trainers and lay down on the bed. Her chest still hurt, but she was fairly sure that nothing was broken. She took deep breaths, until the pain faded and the room started to slip away into silence.

But as she was falling asleep, Sam thought she heard Maddie say something. 'You can only fall in love once.'

Yes, thought Sam. Only once. After that it's all relationships.

Whatever that means.

In the 'morning', when she woke, Maddie was gone. Sam showered, but decided to skip her run – her chest was still hurting, and her ribcage was covered in blue-black bruises. She dressed in jeans, check shirt and an arctic white sweater – hardly stylish, but warm – and went to the console room. There was no sign of the Doctor or Maddie. The scanner showed a grey-black sea, white caps; on the other side, a heath, scruffy grass, a low dawn light.

There was a yellow sticky on the console: 'Gone to the library to do some research. Back in ten minutes.'

Sam frowned. Hadn't the Doctor been going to do that last night? Perhaps, as far as he was concerned, it still was last night. She went through the tall doors into the main part of the library, scanned the rows of shelves that retreated into a misty distance.

A soft footfall behind her made her jump.

'Hello,' said the Doctor. 'I think I've found some of what I'm looking for, but I'll need to check it in the county library to be certain.'

'County library?'

'Yes, well, that's where the local records are kept. I need to know who's living here.'

'Where's "here"?'

'Ramsgate.'

Sam felt the beginnings of a familiar irritation. The Doctor was getting better at explaining what he was doing – but not much better.

'Why –' she began.

'It's where Maddie wanted me to drop her off. She has family here. And she agreed to try and find our friends the Total Liberation Brigade for us. She said she'd leave a message in the county library if she found out anything useful. Since I would be looking in any case.'

Sam had to smile. 'Sounds like a number sixty-seven to me.'

The Doctor gave her one of his big wavy grins. 'Yes! That's it! Leave notes in the same place every week –'

'– until you have something to say, then leave the note –'

'– in a different place!' The Doctor jumped into the air, and for a moment Sam thought he was going to turn a cartwheel: then he seemed to think better of it. 'That's just what I told her to do.'

'Now all we have to do –'

'– is hope it works!'

He took her hand, and they walked back to the console room like that, hand in hand, old friends, and the calendar ticking away the days until the end of the world.

Chapter Sixteen

'One day,' said Jin-Ming, 'There will be no armies. The People's Committees will decide everything.'

Fitz stared out across the dry, hot concrete airfield, trying to suppress a feeling of confusion and distaste. He could hear shouting, the steady tramp of booted feet. All the things that were supposed to be in the past. He knew that the People's Republic needed to defend itself, but this was somehow too much like the old world, the world of military certainty and improper cynicism. And what was he? An agent. An agent of a foreign power, acting against his own country. Like something out of a spy film.

But he *wasn't* a spy. He *believed* in the Revolution.

Didn't he?

The tramping feet got closer, and Fitz could see them: young men in dull-green uniforms, faces bright with sweat, feet rising and falling in a rhythmic dance whose choreography was as old as stone walls and iron spears.

He turned to Jin-Ming. 'I hope that the day of no armies will come soon,' he said.

'Sooner than you think.' Jin-Ming grinned abruptly, and slapped Fitz on the shoulder. 'Let me show you how.'

He led the way across the dull concrete towards a metal guard hut. He exchanged a brief word with the soldier outside, who let them in with a starched salute that was far too much like that of the guards at Buckingham Palace for Fitz's approval. Inside, it was unbelievably hot, like the inside of an oven, and almost dark. Eventually Fitz's eyes adjusted to the gloom as he was led through a maze of passageways, lit by occasional bulbs.

At last he found himself in something like a classroom: long wooden benches with rows of stools. There was even a chalk board, covered in what Fitz at first assumed was Chinese calligraphy.

On closer examination, it was a wiring diagram.

Underneath the diagram was an English word, in crude chalk capitals: B O M B.

For the first time since he'd come to China, Fitz felt the need for a cigarette.

Jin-Ming gestured cheerfully at the board. 'Theory, theory is all very well. But we need to practise, eh?' He unlocked a wooden wall cabinet at the back of the room, and took out wooden box, with two compartments and a sliding lid. It looked like a box for chess pieces. Jin-Ming walked over to Fitz and flipped up the lid. Inside was a metal panel with a clock, and a couple of switches.

'The first switch starts the clock,' said Jin-Ming. 'It sends a detonating pulse every five minutes. The second switch arms the bomb. So you can choose to let it off after five minutes, or two, or one. Clever!'

Fitz stared at the box, confused. His hands began to shake.

'Bomb?' he asked.

'They intend to hit the capitalists. Enemies of the Revolution. Don't worry, it won't be your responsibility. And it's only a small bomb anyway. It's what we get in return that matters.'

'But surely our way is peaceful co-operation and –'

Jin-Ming stared into his eyes. 'For the good of the Revolution,' he said quietly.

Helplessly, Fitz nodded –
– *for the good of the Revolution* –
Jin-Ming flipped the lid closed on the metal box.

The funeral was well attended. Some of the mourners were in black leather jackets, and most were Ed's friends.

Maddie watched them warily, noting the changes that had taken place over the years. Most seemed older, heavier. The men were bearded, the women pale. Many of them had tight, closed expressions, faces that looked away. Their eyes darted around looking for gain, or perhaps for escape. For the first time, under that cold grey March sky, Maddie became aware that something had gone wrong with the revolution, with the name of Love. While she had been searching for mysteries on another continent, these people had lost faith in themselves.

Inside the church, a division became apparent. On one side sat Turton's family: respectable, solemn, the mother puffy-eyed, a few children. On the other, the rock stars and fallen flower children, dark and uneasy.

Maddie joined the latter. At Ed's memorial service she'd sat with the friends because she wanted to. This time, she hardly knew the family, so she didn't have much choice. But then, she hardly knew the friends any more, either.

The 'Brothers Sunshine' were there. In their dark suits they looked like twin chess pieces, black rooks stalking the marbled squares of the nave. They settled in chairs, nesting.

'Hey! Here!'

Maddie turned, saw a familiar face: Fred Hayes – 'Haystacks'. With a shock, she realised that he was one of the people she was here to meet.

The TLB. The Doctor. The end of the world, that was supposed to be happening.

Haystacks was patting a seat next to him, a friendly grin on his face. He looked more normal, more the person she had known, than most of the others, but there was a more serious, adult look on his face nonetheless. He'd been the joker of the company, back then: now he was –

Well, he was a member of an anarchist group who were doing pretty dangerous things in the name of freedom, so what did she expect?

'Hi,' she said.

'Hi.'

The organ started to play then, and everyone stood up. The service was quite long – there were two hymns – and the priest made a veiled reference to the evils of drugs. Some of the assembled flower children looked quite uncomfortable. One laughed at an inopportune moment, and got poisonous glances from the family. Maddie found herself spending most of her time examining the ceiling rosettes, which were painted as bouquets of spring and summer flowers. It seemed a better way to remember Ron, she thought, and to dream of heaven.

At last it was over. Maddie walked out with Haystacks into the cold March air, but couldn't think of anything to say. 'I've heard you're a member of an anarchist group and I'd like to join'? Hardly. She began to see some of the flaws in the Doctor's plan.

'Remember Ed's memorial service?' said Haystacks suddenly.

Maddie nodded, swallowed. 'Yes.' There hadn't been a funeral: they'd never found the body.

'You two were close, weren't you?'

Maddie nodded, looked down across the churchyard, the pale stones. 'I sort of... I suppose I worshipped him, in a way. I've had another boyfriend since, but it wasn't the same.'

Haystacks nodded. He smelled of aftershave: it was over-sweet, almost a perfume. He too was looking across the churchyard. He frowned, then said, 'He said you'd be here.'

It was Maddie's turn to frown. Was Fitz back in England, then? She felt a sense of comfort at the idea – Fitz was strange, but he'd looked after her.

'He said I could tell you. That you could see him.'

'Why didn't he just call? And how does he know you?'

'You don't know the situation with Ed now. He broke his back doing that stunt at the end of the concert. People died. He went into hiding in our basement.'

Maddie blinked, confused. 'You're talking about Ed? Ed's *alive*?'

'Yes. Ed.' He took her arm, squeezed it. 'Who did you think I was talking about?'

Maddie stuttered. 'I thought – I meant – what's he been –'

Haystacks lowered his voice to a murmur. 'He's been living in the basement of our house in East Cheam. He wants to see you because he has a plan. An opportunity to liberate the world. And he wants you to help him.'

Maddie blinked. Whatever she'd expected, she hadn't expected this.

'Oh,' she said.

Maddie hadn't imagined that Ed would be fat.

But he was. He was huge, fat and hairy, a beefsteak of a man with pitted skin and deep, ugly eyes. There was a smell, a sweet odour of incense – but heavily corrupted, as if it were covering something intestinal and putrid. Maddie could almost believe that, under the leather jacket and blue jeans, Ed's body was rotting away in front of her.

For a moment she felt nothing at all: no shock, no fear, nothing except a mild distaste. She was aware of Haystacks beside her, silent, perhaps waiting for a reaction, of the low roof of the cellar room, of a light bulb above a table stacked with newspapers, of cuttings and posters covering the walls.

Then Ed spoke. 'Hi, baby. Long time no see.'

His voice hadn't changed. This crocodilian monster was the man she had made love to. The body slouched and bloated in front of her, corpse-like, was the one that had moved against hers, held her in its arms. She felt vomit rising in her throat, swallowed frantically and got herself under control.

'Aren't you going to talk to me, baby?'

'I'm just –' Maddie swallowed again – 'surprised to see you. I thought you were –'

'Dead?' A strange laugh, a laugh she'd never heard before, more like a series of animal grunts than anything human. 'I'm dead to the world. But I'm still working to change things. It's just the music – the music wasn't doing it. They listened. They listened but they didn't follow.' His face contorted, darkened with blood. 'They didn't do what I told them! And now look!'

A hand, white and puny on the end of an arm like a zeppelin, extended to point at the walls of the cellar room. Maddie looked at the press cuttings, the photographs, the posters. She saw a man being shot by firing squad, a child screaming under a rain of bombs. Headlines: 'WAR…'

'...FAMINE...' 'ATTACK...' 'DEATH...'.

'You think you can stop that by waving flowers around and singing pretty songs? Or by mouthing mantras on stage and twanging sitars?' He was shouting now. Even Haystacks, who surely must be used to Ed, took a sharp breath. 'There's only one way to stop it.'

'Ed!' Haystacks's voice was pleading. 'We need to make sure –'

But Haystacks's body was slammed back against the wall, as if Ed had punched him, though the huge man had made no move. Haystacks just stared, slack-jawed.

Ed glanced sideways, at something under the table. A pile of mulched newspapers, spotty with mould. And growing from them –

White leaves. White stems. White flowers.

'Om-Tsor,' she said.

Ed grinned, revealing cracked lips, yellowed teeth. 'An unlimited supply,' he said.

She knew then. Knew who Ed was.

'Yes,' said Ed, reading her face. 'I'm the Revolution Man. Jean-Pierre Rex was doing the job, but he went chicken. To get results you have to go all the way.'

Maddie started to protest, 'You can't – you shouldn't –' Too late she remembered her mission, her supposed undercover status.

Ed just grinned more widely. A newspaper lifted from the pile on the table and floated unsteadily across the room, as if an invisible man were carrying it. With a sound like a gunshot, the newspaper ripped itself into shreds, which whirled in the air, crackling wildly, and then were suddenly on fire.

'Ed!' bawled Haystacks.

The room was filling with smoke.

Maddie backed away, up the wooden stairs that led down from the cellar door. Behind her, the door flew open. A whirlwind of sparks and fumes rushed past her, and she fell, hard.

She sat up slowly, shaken, coughing. She was on the floor of the cellar. The carpet felt damp, and smelled of vomit. There was still a thin haze of smoke in the cellar, slowly dissipating.

Ed was above her, his chair bewilderingly high. She saw that it had wheels: of course, he couldn't get up. Just for a moment an illusion of perspective showed her his face almost as it had used to be, and she recognized him. Then the chair – which was floating in the air – lowered itself to the ground.

'"The hearts and minds of the people". That's what the napalm-bombers say.' Ed's voice was a low rumble. 'That's what you have to do.'

Maddie, still shaking, stood up. 'I don't think –' She turned and ran towards the door.

It slammed in her face.

She felt a pain in the centre of her forehead, felt herself turn around without having willed it.

'I tried to repair my spine, with Om-Tsor. Made myself real small and tried to put the nerves back in shape. I couldn't, of course. You can't do that. But I read up on it. Nerves, brains. Why people do what they do. It's interesting.'

The pain in Maddie's head intensified. The room seemed wavy, light, the walls fading away.

'I can reach into people's minds and change them, Maddie,' whispered Ed. 'Nobody else can do that. I can save the world.'

Maddie could feel her head shifting, as if her brain was being pulled around inside her skull. The pain was spreading like flames. She tried to scream, tried to look for Haystacks, but her eyes were filling with white light.

The pure white light of the mountains.

And Ed was walking amongst the mountains, just like a god, a god with a shining guitar slung over his shoulder. And that was when Maddie saw the truth of it: Ed was the Revolution Man. Ed would make the Revolution complete.

Ed would become a god, and everything would be all right.

Chapter Seventeen

The road to the border was long, rough and hot, and the suspension on the truck was primitive. Fitz had several bruises by the time they reached the first stop. While the soldiers went outside and smoked Western cigarettes they weren't supposed to have, Fitz tried to fix up a harness from a coil of rope stowed behind the driver's cab.

A footstep on the metal floor made him jump. 'Trying to hang yourself?'

It was Jin-Ming, of course. Fitz laughed. 'Trying to make a harness. But it's no good.' He ran the coarse fibre through his hands. 'I'll just get rope burn instead of bruises.'

Jin-Ming grinned. 'Never mind, it isn't much further.' They were going to the railway station at Chongqing where Fitz was to transfer to a passenger train, and thus Peking and a plane to Paris. Fitz still wasn't sure why he wasn't flying direct to London: it was something to do with customs.

Customs, and the bomb he was carrying in an attaché case, disguised as part of a chess set.

'You remember your friend, that you told us about?' said Jin-Ming suddenly.

Fitz frowned, felt a drop of sweat trickle down his nose. 'Who?'

'The Doctor? The space- and time-traveller? Remember? We didn't believe you!'

Fitz nodded. He remembered them not believing. There had been shouts of laughter, and more pain –

– *a pain between his eyes* –

– for the good of the Revolution –

Fitz blinked. Jin-Ming was wiping at the sweat on his face and his wrist. 'It turns out that one of our new allies in London has a way of contacting the Doctor.'

Fitz felt a shock travel through his body, as if he'd been kicked. The Doctor was around? In London? Now?

A young soldier appeared at the tailgate, barked an instruction in Chinese to Jin-Ming. Fitz caught the word 'start'.

Jin-Ming ignored the interruption. He poked Fitz in the arm, grinned broadly. 'We've also had confirmation from the highest of sources – that's from Chairman Mao Zedong himself! – that the Doctor is real, that his power could also be real. If Chairman Mao can find out how the Doctor travels through time and space...' He broke off, spread his arms, as if to include a whole universe of possibilities. 'We could introduce the Revolution in the fourteenth century! Or the fourth! Think about that – so many generations saved from meaningless exploitation!'

Fitz thought about it for a moment. He looked down at his borrowed Army boots, remembered that the English shoes he'd been wearing were borrowed too – from the Doctor, from the TARDIS. Remembered the money he'd spent getting himself and Maddie to Nepal. The bonds, the stocks, the interest rates.

'I don't think that the Doctor will agree,' he said to Jin-Ming at last. 'He should. But I think he shows –' Fitz struggled for the right words – 'a bourgeois dialectic. He has a tendency to display individualism, even –' Fitz hesitated – 'entrepreneurism.'

'So you think the Doctor is a capitalist, and you're not

sure you'll be able to persuade him to change his ways?' Jin-Ming had a crafty smile on his face.

Fitz nodded.

'Close your eyes.'

Fitz closed them. He heard a rustle of fabric, then felt cold metal pressed into his hand. He opened his eyes, saw that he was holding a revolver.

'This will help you persuade the Doctor,' said Jin-Ming, smiling. 'If all else fails!' He winked. 'Come on, the truck will wait for us.' He patted the gun in Fitz's hand. 'I will show you how to use it.'

The hovercraft terminal at Ramsgate had an abandoned air to it. A concrete apron, floodlit, was whipped by frothy, translucent waves. Low buildings with bright windows stood next to a car park, an expanse of bare asphalt grey-white under grey-blue clouds. A single small red car moved across it, apparently purposeless, perhaps lost.

Sam stood, shivering a little, in the cold wind whipping in from the sea, watching the horizon for any sign of the incoming craft. Somewhere beyond her sight, a NATO fleet was heading across the North Sea towards a naval exercise in the Baltic, to be performed only just outside Soviet waters. The world was becoming a dangerous place – right on schedule. It was only five weeks before the Doctor's deadline. But from the headlines in the paper Sam had bought, it was hard to believe that it was going to be even that long. Extra US troops were being shipped to Europe. Russian tanks were on manoeuvres in East Germany.

Maddie's message had arrived on the Doctor's tenth visit to Ramsgate library. 'TLB about to bomb US Embassy using

Chinese bomb – need your help. Meet 9 a.m. on 12th April, Ramsgate Hoverport.'

It didn't take much savvy to work out the consequences if the bomb was used, and traced back to its source, in the present situation.

A booming sound echoed over the sea, varying so much in volume that it sounded almost like some alien variation of the TARDIS materialisation noises. Sam decided that it had to be the hovercraft. It sounded horribly inefficient, yet she remembered that sixties' science fiction had been full of futures with hovercraft. They obviously hadn't thought about the energy budget.

She watched the curve of spray that marked the position of the craft as it crawled across the water, and wondered what it would be like to meet Maddie again. Two months of Maddie's time had passed to only a day of Sam's. Sam knew how much it was possible to change in just a couple of months – her first weeks in the TARDIS, for instance, or the first weeks on Ha'olam. She began making her way down the cliff path: as she did so, she noticed that people were emerging from the terminal. A queue of cars began moving down the road in front of her: one stopped to let her cross. On the other side she almost ran into Maddie.

She had changed: her face seemed firmer, more serious, and the expression in her eyes was wary. Her hair was tied up in a bun.

'Sam! I'm glad you got here in time!'

Sam frowned. 'I thought you were on –' she gestured at the hovercraft, now manoeuvring noisily towards the apron.

Maddie said something that Sam didn't catch over the

noise of the engines.

'What was that?' she asked.

Maddie raised her voice, but the engines were even louder now and all Sam heard was: '...agent... craft... Om... bee!'

Sam cupped her hands and shouted. 'What agent?'

Maddie too cupped her hands and shouted. 'There's a Chinese secret agent on the hovercraft. He's come to get Om-Tsor from the TLB. I'm meant to be showing him to the house in London.'

Sam looked at the lumbering craft, now making its way in a welter of spray and bright black rubber out of the sea. The passenger cabins looked tiny.

'Why didn't he fly in?' bawled Sam.

'It's easier to get through customs here. Or something.'

Sam wondered about that. What was the agent carrying, that customs procedures would make a difference? There was one obvious answer. But why smuggle it in this way? And anyway, why would the Chinese want to supply arms to a tin-pot Anarchist group?

'What are the TLB giving the Chinese in return?' she bawled at Maddie.

Maddie looked away, shook her head.

Om-Tsor, thought Sam. It has to be Om-Tsor. But where are they getting it from? We're no nearer knowing that than we were a year ago.

The craft had finally settled in the bay, and after an interval the engines stopped and the load bay door opened. As cars streamed out, the increasingly familiar sixties smell of unburned petrol and oil filled the air.

A blue car stopped suddenly – so suddenly that there was

a screech of tyres as the car behind pulled up, followed by the blare of a horn. Then the car started up again, but moving more slowly. Sam saw a face staring at her from the driver's seat. The skin was tanned, the brown hair cut neat and short, well above the collar of a smart business suit. But there was something familiar about the shifty grey eyes.

Fitz.

What the –

But the car was in the queue for the exit, the driver out of sight.

Maddie touched her arm. 'What is it?'

'I think I just saw Fitz.'

Maddie bit her lip. 'Er – that's – um – possible.'

Before Sam could ask for an explanation, Maddie turned and ran, towards the stream of passengers now emerging from the terminal. Sam followed, feeling the strong wind catch her body as she ran against it. They were both brought up short by the sheer number of people, and the customs barrier.

'Entrance round that way, miss!' shouted someone, but Sam didn't take any notice.

'Why is it possible?'

'Fitz is the agent,' said Maddie. 'And before you ask, I don't know. OK? I don't know why they're using him, except he's English I suppose. And he doesn't know you're here – at least, I don't think so.'

'Well, he'll know in a minute,' said Sam. 'Unless I hide.'

Maddie shook her head. 'It'll be OK. But let me do the talking, right?'

Sam seriously doubted that this would be possible, but she nodded anyway, searching the other woman's face for clues. *Something* was wrong. Something had happened in the last two months. If Fitz was a Chinese agent… It was ridiculous. How *could* he be? She reminded herself that if she'd missed two months of Maddie's life in the last day, she'd missed nigh-on two *years* of Fitz's in no more than a week. Anything could have happened.

But surely he'd have more sense than to work for the Chinese?

A rather tired-looking man in rumpled casual clothes pushed his way past Sam with a muttered, 'Excuse me – we're late'. A woman followed, dark-haired, pulling a grinning child. There was confusion at the gate as they tried to get in through the exit. The woman protested – 'I want you to get my car! *I* can't drive it on *there*!' The child grinned more broadly and jumped up and down with excitement.

Self-centred little brat, thought Sam. Who'd have children?

She saw Fitz then, waving a passport at a customs official. He looked authoritative in a smart business suit, with a briefcase and an umbrella. All he needed was a bowler hat and he'd be John Steed. Well, he was a bit younger, maybe. And a bit more tanned…

Sam decided to play it cool. Maddie had said she'd do the talking – let her.

Fitz had reached the exit barrier by now. It went up, and he and the briefcase went through. Sam watched his face, saw the weathering there. He looked five years older, not two. She glanced sidelong at Maddie, saw a similar reaction of shock, and decided that it was China that had aged Fitz.

He was holding out his hands to Maddie. 'Maddie – what –'

'She has to be here. I'll explain in a minute.'

Fitz was looking increasingly confused. 'I was told that you would be meeting me.'

He sounded pompous and official. Sam wondered for a moment if he was putting it on. But there seemed to be no trace of humour in his face, no hint of the self-deprecating, if somewhat insecure, young man she'd known. It was as if somebody had wiped his character away with a sponge, leaving only the etched-in outlines of his face, hard and without any particular interest in the world.

He smiled at her. 'I'm happy now, Sam. I don't want to go back to the TARDIS. I never did. I have Maddie, and I have – political beliefs. Please go away.'

Brainwashing, thought Sam. She remembered stories of captured American soldiers in the Korean war, subjected to sensory deprivation, torture, bawled insults, until they half-believed in the Revolution. But hadn't those stories been proved untrue? You couldn't brainwash someone against their will, whatever you did to them.

But perhaps it depended on how much will they had to start with. Fitz had always seemed indecisive, unsure, almost neurotic at times – his cheap showing off, his addictions, his attempts to avoid a crisis rather than face up to it. Perhaps he'd needed a centre to his life – and now one had been offered to him.

Fitz and Maddie started to walk along the promenade, past the car park, away from the terminal. Sam followed them, keeping a slight distance, hoping they would speak. They were walking hand-in-hand, and Maddie was glancing up at Fitz from time to time, moving her face towards him as if trying for a kiss. Fitz, however, just walked on in silence. Eventually Maddie let go of his hand.

It was odd, Sam decided, for lovers who'd just met up again to act this way. There was definitely something very wrong with Fitz. And Maddie seemed curiously unresentful. Sam felt like striding forward and asking them both what was going on. A year ago, she probably would have done. But now, some detective instinct made her hang back, wait, listen.

'Sam!'

The Doctor's voice. Sam cursed inwardly.

'I think I've found – oh!'

He'd obviously seen Fitz.

'Oh, *no*!'

He obviously didn't think it was a good development.

Fitz had seen the Doctor, now, was staring over his shoulder. He grabbed Maddie's arm, dragged her into a run. Sam heard Maddie's protesting voice – 'It's all right!' – but she went with him. Sam saw the blue car, a man in the uniform of the hovercraft company waving at Fitz as he got out of the driver's seat.

Sam hesitated, and by then it was too late. The car swerved across the car park, tyres squeaking – then it was on the road and away.

The Doctor arrived at her elbow. Unusually, he sounded a little out of breath: Sam wondered how far he'd been running. 'What's happening?' he asked.

'I wish I knew,' said Sam. 'I don't understand it at all.'

Fitz was angry. Maddie was sure of it, even though he was smiling, even though his tanned face was alien, remote.

'We agreed,' she said, feeling desperate – and too young for this, much too young. 'We said we would get the Doctor

215

for you.'

'It should have been a meeting under controlled circumstances.' Fitz shook his head. 'I'm sorry, Maddie. My original instructions didn't include this. I'm not sure we can make it work. I told them that in China –' he broke off. 'How did they know about the Doctor?'

Maddie's face twisted. 'I told – them.'

Fitz spotted the hesitation. He'd always been quick like that. 'Told who? The TLB?'

Maddie nodded, relieved that he hadn't thought she was talking about a specific person. Let Fitz suspect she was working for more than one organisation. Let him even think she was still helping the Doctor. Let him think anything but the truth.

White light drifted in the corners of her vision. Air moved near her ear.

'Where are you going, Maddie?' said Ed's voice. 'We need the Doctor and his machine, not this clown and his bomb. Get inside the TARDIS. I don't care how you do it.'

I can't help it, thought Maddie furiously, though Ed couldn't always hear her thoughts. She wished she hadn't involved Fitz. She'd told Ed that the Doctor would come without the excuse of the bomb, but Ed hadn't believed it. He'd wanted a backup – someone he could threaten, someone he could convert who knew more about the TARDIS than Maddie did.

Now it seemed he was changing his mind. Maddie felt a cold, confused, terror. Her hands began shaking.

There was a bang, and the car lurched to one side, hit a grass verge. Road, verge and blue-grey clouds began to spin around the windows.

'Ed!' shrieked Maddie. She saw the doors crumple, the windscreen shatter into white stars of glass. She shut her eyes.

The body of the car jolted, once, then they had stopped.

'That was strange,' said Fitz. His hands were still on the wheel. He looked shaken, but not as deeply shocked as Maddie was expecting. 'The car was lifted up, wasn't it? By someone using Om-Tsor?'

Maddie said nothing.

Fitz reached into his coat, pulled out a silver object –

A *gun*.

'Fitz, I don't think that's a good idea.' Maddie could feel Ed's breath moving in the car, like a divine wind, but smelling of the London cellar. A pale green car was pulling up behind them, indicator blinking, the driver waving at them and smiling. It seemed absurd, like a sketch from a TV comedy show.

There was a snap, like a stick breaking, and Fitz howled with pain. The gun spun in the air, bounced off the roof, landed in Maddie's lap.

She picked it up, but there was no need to aim it at Fitz. His body was pressed back against the driver's door of the car. A red welt was forming across his throat, and his face was turning blue.

'Ed!' whispered Maddie desperately. 'We need him!'

'No we don't. Not alive, anyway. He's been tampered with already – I can't use him. Just get inside the TARDIS. You know what to do.'

Fitz began to struggle, but his limbs only jerked feebly. He was as helpless as a fly in a spider's web. Maddie sat there with the gun in her lap, watching him die. She wanted to move her hands, to help him, to call out, but she couldn't. There was a white light in her mind, holding it in place.

Chapter Eighteen

Even before they reached the TARDIS, the Doctor started to run again. Sam was barely able to keep up. Her ribs were still painful, and her left foot must have been bruised in her brush with the Revolution Man: it hurt every time she put it down.

'Hey,' she called after him as they pounded across the short grass. 'Wait for me!'

'No time!' bawled the Doctor. He was already at the TARDIS, struggling with the door. By the time Sam got inside he was at the console, flicking switches. The TARDIS began to dematerialise.

The console room was a mess. There were several book trolleys from the local library, and what looked like a filing trolley hung with a mass of folded paper and punch cards. Scraps of paper were all over the floor, and draped over the side of the VW Beetle and the motorcycle which seemed to have taken up residence by its side.

'Whatever you do, don't leave the TARDIS!' yelled the Doctor suddenly.

Sam looked at the closed door, then at the blank scanner screens, then at the Doctor. The expression on his face was serious. 'Where are we going to land?' she asked.

As if in answer, the TARDIS stopped with a jolt. A clock chimed: a metal object, perhaps a paint tin lid, rattled on the floor a few times and then was silent.

The doors flew open, and the Doctor all but flew out of them.

'Stay inside!' he bawled over his shoulder.

Sam looked at the scanner. She could see a grass verge, and a battered-looking blue car parked against it, tilted slightly. The Doctor was struggling with the driver's door, then with something inside the car. Lights flashed around him, as if somebody was directing low-intensity laser fire at his body. Sam looked around, wondering about marauding aliens, but saw only cars travelling up and down a dual carriageway.

There was a pale green car parked behind the crashed one, with a man slumped over the bonnet. Sam saw blood leaking from his body.

She almost rushed from the TARDIS, then remembered the Doctor's instructions. He was running back now, with a stumbling Fitz – *Fitz!* – in tow.

'Everyone! Inside!' bawled the Doctor. He was nearly at the TARDIS door, but he seemed to be fighting a gale. The flashing lights made a teardrop shape around him, hiding his body and Fitz's.

Someone else was getting out of the car – Maddie, of course. 'Stop!' she was shouting, but at who or what, Sam wasn't sure.

The Doctor had made it to the TARDIS doors – she could see his face, his body straining as if he were dragging a boulder. The TARDIS shuddered as he came through, Fitz staggering after him.

As they pushed past her, Sam saw Maddie on the road, perhaps five metres away, a pleading expression on her face. She too was trying to run against the wind, but didn't appear to be making any headway.

'Doctor!' shouted Sam. But the Doctor was flicking

switches on the console. Fitz was slumped against one of the support pillars, gasping.

Sam leaned out of the door as far as she dared, hanging on to the lintel. A huge force punched into her body, pushing her back.

Maddie was closer.

Sam leaned out again, and this time Maddie made it to within an arm's length of the TARDIS. Sam reached out, grabbed her, and hauled her in.

The doors slammed shut.

The TARDIS trembled, and began to dematerialise.

Maddie grabbed Sam's arm. 'We've got to go to London!' she stage-whispered. 'The house in –'

'– East Cheam.' The Doctor was looking at them over the console, his expression alert, inquiring. 'I know. But before we go there I think we need to make some preparations.'

Fitz clutched the briefcase containing the bomb against his shins and wondered how close he had come to dying.

Too close, he decided. The world had been fading away, there hadn't even been any pain left. Another few seconds –

His throat hurt like hell. He looked at Maddie, talking rapidly to Sam under the dark arch of the doorway. Why hadn't she helped him?

The Doctor kneeled down by his side. 'Are you all right, Fitz?'

Fitz nodded. He didn't want to speak to the Doctor at the moment. The serious, boyish yet adult face, the halo-like frame of hair, seemed too familiar, as if he'd only left the TARDIS yesterday. Recognition was clogging his thought processes, and he needed to think. His original mission – to obtain the source of Om-Tsor – was in considerable jeopardy. It was obvious that someone within the TLB was able to use the drug in a very controlled and powerful way, and wasn't afraid to kill. Perhaps it was the Revolution Man himself, perhaps someone else who was buying from him, or even supplying him. Whichever, Fitz didn't see how this person would give any of the drug up to him in return for a bomb which was little more than a grenade in a fancy box. Let alone trade him the secret of its source. So why had the mission been arranged?

Fitz realised that either Jin-Ming had been lying to him, or that the man simply hadn't the faintest idea what he was doing. But the orders regarding the Doctor had come directly from Mao himself. Which meant –

The Doctor, still kneeling beside him, coughed gently. 'Perhaps you need to sleep.'

Fitz jumped. He'd forgotten the Doctor was there. Before Fitz could gather his wits, he'd lifted Fitz's case from by his side and put it on what appeared to be a library book trolley. It teetered for a moment, and Fitz held his breath, though he knew the bomb wouldn't detonate under any normal impact. He wondered if the Doctor had a bomb detector in the TARDIS. The device was supposed to be advanced, and almost undetectable, but Fitz doubted it would fool the Doctor.

The best thing would be if he didn't take a look. And the easiest way to ensure that was for Fitz to pretend to be on his side.

Weapons, duplicity, uncertainty, thought Fitz unhappily. I'm back in the capitalist world all right. Worse, I'm not even sure I trust the people who sent me any more.

'Oh, no!' The Doctor's voice made Fitz jump. 'Sam! I need you to help me here!'

Sam rushed past Fitz, all but tripping over him. Fitz struggled to his feet, ignoring pain in his throat and a wave of dizziness. He staggered to the console, saw the familiar white figures of the calendar wheeling forward.

'There must be a slippage in the vortex!' the Doctor was saying. 'The instability is too great!' He suddenly dived *under* the console, muttering something about positive inductance feedback.

The dizziness returned, and Fitz almost fell against the console. A switch moved under his hand, and there was a grinding sound from the time rotor, as if it was jamming against broken glass.

With a shock that almost jolted Fitz on to the floor, the TARDIS stopped.

The Doctor was on his feet again. 'Well done, Fitz!' He clapped Fitz on the shoulder. 'It's nice to know the TARDIS still likes you.' The Doctor smiled at him, one of his meaningful smiles, and Fitz realised that he could feel a presence in his head, a gentle modulation of his thoughts that he recognised from two years before.

I could've done with the TARDIS in China with everyone babbling in dialect around me, he thought. *I might have had a better idea what was going on*.

'Oh, dear,' said the Doctor. The remark appeared to be addressed to the console. The Doctor was staring at the calendar. Fitz forced himself to concentrate, saw that the date read: '18 May 1969'.

'So?' he asked.

'The world ends today,' whispered the Doctor. '*Today*.' He

223

whirled round, grabbed Fitz by the arm, marched him around the console to where Sam was standing, staring at a screen and shaking her head.

'We're in London,' she said. 'But where is everyone?'

Fitz glanced at the screen, saw empty suburban streets. 'What day of the week is it?'

'Sunday,' said the Doctor. 'But even so –'

Maddie joined them at the console. 'That's the house! We've got to get to the house!'

'Maddie, it's not that simple any more,' began the Doctor. 'We may already be too late.'

Maddie grabbed his arm. 'We've got to get to the house! The Revolution Man will be in there!'

'Why?' snapped the Doctor. 'How do you know?'

Maddie said nothing, but her face darkened in a blush. 'He's –' she began, then tried again, 'It's –'

The Doctor looked at the screen again. There was still no movement in the street outside. The Doctor swung round and grabbed Fitz by the shoulders. 'What was Mao offering them for the use of Om-Tsor? A bomb? Have you got it with you?'

Fitz swallowed, then cautiously nodded. 'I've got something they might want. But I'm not sure if –'

'Will you go in there, see what's happening. If anyone will talk to you, of course. We have to know what the situation is now, not what it was six weeks ago.' He slapped the console, and the doors opened. 'Maddie, I want to talk to you.'

Fitz went to the doors. Rather to his surprise, Sam trotted after him. 'You need backup,' she said, simply. 'And I know the house. I've been there before.'

He glanced at her, seeing her properly for the first time. She hadn't changed at all in the two years he'd been away. Even her hair looked the same. But there was something in her face he hadn't seen before, though it had probably been there: a calmness, a maturity.

She reached out a hand. Fitz took hold of it, squeezed it briefly.

Outside, it was hot, a dry May heat under a sky glazed white with thin, high clouds. Fitz heard the distant sound of traffic, which was reassuring, and a voice on a radio or television, speaking in solemn tones. He heard the word 'war', and glanced at Sam, but she didn't seem to be listening. She was counting houses along the street.

'This way,' she said suddenly.

Fitz followed her, starting to sweat in the heavy coat he'd been wearing for Ramsgate on a cold April morning. He began to feel some of the thrill and bewilderment of time travel. It reminded him of the very first time he'd seen the TARDIS interior, unexpectedly huge, like a cross between a cathedral, an Art Deco sculpture park and a Victorian drawing room, with bits of car park and library thrown in for good measure. He'd missed it, hadn't he, while he'd been with Maddie. The world had been ordinary again. Perhaps that was why he'd agreed to go to Nepal.

'Here,' said Sam, making an abrupt left along a path through a garden gone wild and weedy, buzzing with insects. A tattered door with peeling green paint and a stripe of candy yellow.

When Sam knocked, it opened slightly under the impacts. She pushed it back, looked around.

Fitz pushed forward, looked over her shoulder, saw empty

rooms. A can of paint. There was a smell of something rotting. Sam went in, calling out. There was no response, just the dead echo of an empty house.

'We're too late,' said Fitz.

Sam was ahead of him somewhere. 'There's a cellar,' she said. 'We never saw the cellar before – ugh!'

Fitz caught up with her, peered down a flight of dim wooden steps into darkness. 'I hate cellars,' he said, with feeling. The smell was revolting, as if an animal had died in there. A large one. He was glad when Sam produced a small torch from a side pocket of her backpack and went down first.

He saw newspapers, ashes, leery shadows.

'Nothing,' reported Sam. She shone the torch around. There were no bolt holes, nor any signs of recent habitation. Under the table was a blackened heap of ash.

'So where have they gone?' he asked.

'Let's get back to the TARDIS. Maddie was working with them for a couple of months. She must know something.'

'I don't think –' began Fitz, then stopped abruptly. He'd been going to tell Sam that he wasn't sure they could trust Maddie, that she'd sat there and watched him being strangled – but then he remembered something else from that moment.

The gun in her lap.

The gun that wasn't in the holster inside his coat any more.

Sam was watching him, a frown on her face.

'Sam,' he said quietly. 'Maddie has a gun.'

They stared at each other for a moment, then set off at a run for the street.

It was hot, it was silent, it was empty.

The TARDIS was gone.

Then the radio or television commentary started up again. It was louder this time, and Fitz could hear the words clearly.

'Unless there is a miracle,' said the announcer. 'We are now counting down the minutes to the Third World War.'

Chapter Nineteen

Maddie closed her eyes, reached again into the strange infinity of mazes that was the geometry of the TARDIS. But it was no good. The Om-Tsor showed her things, but she had no idea what the things were, or what to do with them.

She opened her eyes, saw that the Doctor was still watching her. She'd tied him to his armchair with a rope she'd found, gagged him in case there was anyone else living in the TARDIS and he tried to call for help. Now she had to ungag him, to get some answers out of him.

'You're going to have to show me what to do.'

'No,' said the Doctor, simply.

She walked up to him, trying to be threatening, wishing that Ed's original plan to use Fitz had worked.

'Look, you said it yourself – the world's coming to an end unless you stop it. So –'

The Doctor raised his eyebrows. 'So let me go and I'll stop it! Look, Maddie, I don't know why you're doing this –'

'You don't need to. Just do as I say. Do as I say and we might be able to save something from the wreck, OK?'

The Doctor seemed to read something in her eyes, in her mind. 'All right,' he said softly. 'We'll do it your way.'

He didn't sound convincing enough for the white light inside Maddie, for the crystallised version of Ed's desires that was nesting in her mind.

'You must follow my instructions,' she said. 'If you don't –' she shifted the gun in her hand – 'I'll have to kill you.'

* * *

'What now?' asked Sam.

'I take it that's rhetorical,' said Fitz, staring around the empty street hoping that a miracle – or better still, the TARDIS – would materialise out of thin air in front of him. 'We don't know where the Om-Tsor is. We don't know where the Revolution Man is or whether he ever existed, we don't know where the Doctor is and the world's going to be blown to pieces in about ten minutes. My instructions didn't cover any of this.'

'Then what did they cover?' snapped Sam. 'Why were you working for them anyway? And why should I trust you now?'

Fitz shrugged. 'It seemed easier. They seemed to have everything under control. Everything was for the good of the people.' He paused. 'I still think it's better. Look what happens if you get individualists in charge of things. The Doctor's not much good in that contraption of his. Imagine the power of the TARDIS in the hands of someone like Mao!'

Sam stared at him. 'You weren't going to –'

Fitz felt a warm blush spreading across his face. He realised that he needed to make her trust him, that they *had* to work together now. 'I – I don't know. But I'm sure that Om-Tsor would be better handled by someone who truly represents the people, rather than –'

'Fitz!' Sam's face was flushed too, perhaps with anger. 'How stupid can you get? You know what the Chinese government is like!'

'Do I? And how would I know that? All I know is that where I was working, everyone was peaceful and happy –'

'I bet they were! What did they call it? "Chairman Mao Model Commune"?'

Fitz swallowed, looked away. 'Erm – something like that,' he agreed.'And I suppose the military –' He remembered the old monk, dead. Had Jin-Ming done that? How had he forgotten?

He closed his eyes, heard Jin-Ming's voice.

'– for the good of the Revolution –'

Light. And a pain between his eyes.

Om-Tsor.

'They didn't want Om-Tsor to control weapons,' he said suddenly. 'They wanted it to control minds. They thought it would be better that way. Jin-Ming –'

'I just take a little, a little like this, and I can make you understand in the right way. So easy! So clever! No battles and no blood!'

'Jin-Ming must have controlled Maddie – no, that's impossible –'

'Somebody has. She was working for us, watching the TLB. And now –' she gestured at the empty street, the vanished TARDIS.

'And that somebody attacked me in the car when I pulled a gun on Maddie.'

They looked at each other.

'The Revolution Man?' said Sam after a moment.

'Must be.'

There was a silence between them. The slow chant of the Lord's Prayer could be heard on the radio.

'Come on,' said Sam softly. 'Let's see if the neighbours know anything about our absent friends.'

'That house?' said the old lady. 'Oh, they were youngsters. A bad lot. Untidy, noisy.' She peered over her spectacles, smiled at them. A ginger cat appeared and wound itself around her ankles, purring. Behind them, the house looked dark, comforting. 'They've probably gone to that concert.'

'What concert?' asked Sam and Fitz, almost in unison.

'The one at Wembley Stadium! What did they call it? "Rock at the End of the World"? And that pop star came back from the dead – or said he did – you know, personally I believe that only the Lord Jesus Christ can help any of us now –'

'What was the name of the pop star?' interrupted Sam.

The woman blinked at her. 'Oh, I don't know. I tell you, it doesn't matter now. You should pray. It's the only thing that'll save us, whatever they all say.' She paused. 'Ed something, perhaps?'

'Ed Hill? Wasn't that Maddie's boyfriend? The singer in Kathmandu?'

Sam glanced at Fitz, who nodded. 'He vanished from –'

'– a rock concert. And Om-Tsor was involved.'

'So if he's still alive, and using Om-Tsor –'

They stared at each other. Fitz remembered standing above the Earth, looking down on blue land and ocean. Every detail clear to him.

'We could use Om-Tsor to stop the war,' he said. 'Intercept the missiles. Something. There's a chance.'

'We need to get to Wembley.' Sam was off down the path at a run.

Fitz shrugged, thanked the old lady.

'I'll pray for you,' she said.

'Thanks,' said Fitz again. Sam was already half way down the road. He hoped she knew how to get to the stadium. 'We might need it.'

'We're going to *persuade* Ed to let us stop the war?' asked Fitz. 'Is that the best you can come up with?'

It was a free concert, arranged only two days before: even so, the crowds around Wembley were packed tight, and he doubted that they would even be able to get to Ed, let alone persuade him about anything.

'What else can we do?' Sam was shouldering her way through the crowd. 'There's no point in destroying the world, just for the sake of it. He can't have meant to do this.'

Fitz remembered his own past, in the days before the Doctor. The dark pits of cynicism, the near-total despair that sometimes dragged him right under. If things had been a little bit worse – if the Doctor hadn't come along –

'I wouldn't be too sure,' he said aloud.

Sam ignored him, kept pushing her way forward. A woman in a kaftan was staring open-mouthed at the sky. A circle of men in black leather jackets were banging tambourines and doing a shuffling dance. 'Last – chance – to – get – high!' they chanted. Another man was laughing hysterically, kneeling in the middle of the crowd, tears running down his face.

Fitz followed Sam as best he could, keeping the briefcase clutched against to his chest. He hadn't told her about the bomb yet. He was hoping he wouldn't have to use it. But – just as Jin-Ming had warned him, in rather different circumstances – he had to face the fact that persuasion might not be enough.

'This way!' said Sam, making a sudden left turn. For a moment they were battling against the flow of people, then they were up against a metal wire barrier. Beyond it they could see trucks – a removal van, a green lorry with a BBC logo, a couple of drab olive vehicles which reminded Fitz of Army trucks, and a zebra-striped VW camper van.

Sam started to climb the barrier. It swayed dangerously: Fitz had to grab hold of it. There was no way he could climb it as well, or the whole structure might collapse.

But other people were starting on the barrier now. Fitz saw a man with a beard and a shock of golden hair scrambling up, as limber as a chimpanzee. When he reached the top he yelled over his shoulder, 'No more barriers! This is the last day!' and jumped down inside.

Fitz cursed under his breath. This was becoming an incident, and his and Sam's chances of getting anywhere now were remote. Inside the barrier, a heavy-set man in a dark jacket was running across, shouting something. Two policemen were pushing through the crowd behind them. Sam was astride the top of the barrier, yelling 'Come on, Fitz!', which wasn't much help.

Reluctantly, Fitz started to climb. He felt hands grab his legs, try to pull him down. The barrier tilted crazily. There was a clatter of metal, a shout, a few screams. Hands grabbed Fitz's arms, yanked him upwards. He saw the golden-haired man smiling at him.

He scrambled clear, found himself standing inside the barrier, which was now slanting and partly lifted off the ground. Sam was ahead of him, running. Fitz followed, dodging a couple of men in suits, one with a microphone in his hand. Sam was jumping over cables, dodging around the back of the striped camper van and in through a set of double doors. By the time Fitz got there, a policeman was blocking the way.

'I have to get my sister!' snapped Fitz, in his most authoritative tone.

That and the business suit must have done it, or perhaps the policeman saw easier prey: anyway he moved aside, and

Fitz found himself chasing through a passageway.

'Up here!' Sam's voice.

Fitz was climbing stairs, running into a bright, neon-lit passage. 'Are you sure about this?' he called.

Behind them, running footsteps, shouting.

They ran along the passage, up another flight of stairs. At the top, Sam stopped. For the first time he could remember, Fitz heard her swear.

'It's wrong. They must rebuild it – redesign it – before my time. Or something. This should be above the player's entrance.'

Fitz stared at her. She had her back against a green double door with a brass handle, marked 'APPROVED PERSONNEL ONLY'. One half of the door was open, revealing grey sky, black stands, a black pitch.

Black?

He stepped forward, looked out. The stadium was like the inside of a funeral parlour. Everything was draped in black. The stands, the seating, the pitch, were all covered in cloth. The audience, spilling in, had made colours, a slow spread of life across the dark setting.

In the middle of the pitch was the stage. It was a huge black flower, the petals spread out flat. In the centre of the stage a drum kit, amplifiers, and towering speaker stacks made a black pistil and stamens. There was a single spot of white in the middle of it all: after a moment, Fitz realised that it was a man.

Ed Hill. Was he *really* the Revolution Man?

Sam was leaning forward, looking down over a low metal rail. They were on a gantry – for cameras? lights? – attached to a pillar supporting the main roof. It had to be thirty feet down to the seats below.

'There must be a ladder – something –'

Fitz felt a spot of water on his hand, realised it was starting to rain. He looked over his shoulder, saw two policeman and what looked like a bouncer running up the stairs towards them.

'They're here!' he snapped at Sam.

She went over the rail without a word, swung herself on to the pillar. Fitz saw that she was holding on to an iron ladder at the corner between the gantry and the pillar, painted red like the pillar, almost invisible.

'Hey!' he called after Sam. 'I'm not Tarzan, you know!'

Then the doors burst open, and Fitz jumped over the rail without thinking – and without looking. He almost missed the ladder, almost fell. Below him, Sam was scrambling down. Faces from the audience turned upwards, hands reached out to help.

As Fitz landed awkwardly in an aisle, a huge, discordant note roared out from the speakers, drowning all thought and almost bursting Fitz's eardrums.

They started down towards the pitch, towards the stage. People were streaming up the aisle, and though most of the faces were friendly, Fitz and Sam had to fight to make progress. The speakers roared with music, making any conversation impossible.

Ed Hill started to sing.

'I'm back from the dead, baby,
'Back from six feet underground...'

The rest of the words were lost in a roar of cheering from the crowd. Did they really think that a self-proclaimed resurrected singer could save them from World War Three?

At the bottom of the aisle, there was a low wall. Sam and Fitz scrambled over it without any difficulty, but beyond was a sea of people, crammed thick on to the pitch.

Fitz looked at Sam through the wall of sound and mutely shook his head.

Sam made walking gestures with her fingers.

'What?' bawled Fitz.

'Back from the dead, better than before, I'm gonna save you from the Third World War!'

Fitz had to admit, the tune was catchy. And the bass playing was damn good. Even since last summer, music had moved on.

Sam grabbed Fitz's head and shouted in his ear, 'Walk over them! Crocodile Dundee!'

Fitz shook his head in bewilderment. Sam stepped out over the crowd, shouting something down at them. To his amazement, it seemed to work. She was picking her way across the top of the crowd, supported by a hand here, a head there. Fitz followed. It was slow, but it was easier than cramming across at ground level. Twice he fell – once caught a woman in the eye with a flailing hand – but people helped him up and on his way. They seemed to sense he had a mission.

'There's no way out now except to follow Ed, baby,
'Ed, Ed, Ed, who comes back from the dead, baby…'

Sam got further and further ahead. Several other people started to climb across the crowd towards the stage, with varying degrees of success. The rain was falling heavily now, screening the stands in mist. There was a brief pause in the music, and Fitz heard the distant, terrifying wail of air-raid sirens.

* * *

Sam felt the hands on her body, literally shoving her up over the lip of the stage. Ahead, she recognised Haystacks, looking huge and threatening in a black jacket with metal studs, and Pippa, wayward and paranoid, her eyes moving. They fixed on Sam, and she shouted something, inaudible over the pounding bass.

Sam glanced over her shoulder. She couldn't see Fitz – he might be doing anything. She thought about how she'd instinctively just fallen back into trusting Fitz. Maybe that wasn't the wisest thing, but it was too late to stop now. Hands reached up from the crowd to grab her – obviously hoping for a lift on to the stage – so she ran, ran towards the obscene white blob in the middle of the stage that must be Ed Hill.

She noticed that the light was changing and glanced up. The rain had stopped, and a hole was appearing in the clouds. She saw blue sky, streaked with contrails. Jets? Then she saw one being made, saw the terrifying speed of it, and realised the truth.

The air-raid sirens had been for real. The missiles were on their way.

Behind the contrails, a circle of sky was brightening, and inside it, the capital letter R.

Fine, thought Sam. Clever you, clever Revolution Man for starting all this. So how are you going to stop it?

Hands grabbed her arms: Haystacks. Sam cursed herself for taking her attention away from the stage, even for an instant.

'I've got to talk to Ed,' she yelled.

She wasn't sure Haystacks had heard her, even from arm's length.

Ed was singing: '*Back from the dead, better than before, I*

WILL SAVE YOU from the Third World War!'

He started to chant: '*I – WILL – SAVE – YOU –*'

'What's he going to do?' bawled Sam.

'…save us!' bawled Haystacks. '…Tsor!'

'It won't work!' yelled Sam, though she didn't know why. 'He can't do it on his own!'

She struggled, but Haystacks's face was set hard, white flesh running with rainwater. He didn't let her go.

By the time Fitz reached the stage, his legs were aching, his coat was soaked with rain and his business suit was soaked with sweat. His throat hurt, too. As he was levered up, he noticed the Revolution Man symbol in the sky, the contrails crossing it. Lightning flickered somewhere beyond the top of the stands. Sam was still arguing. Ed was chanting. Some people in the crowd had started to scream. How long did anyone have?

'*I – WILL – SAVE – YOU –*'

Fitz recognised the original Om-Tsor mantra, from the Top Thirty hit of 1967. He saw Ed centre stage, and ran across the rain-slick wood, dodging Sam and her captor, heading straight for Ed. He struggled with the catches on his briefcase, ready to pull out the bomb. To show Ed that he wasn't in control, that he, Fitz, was in control and –

'*I – WILL – SAVE – YOU –*'

The music stopped, and Ed's voice boomed through the speakers, 'Actually, my children, *I AM GOD*, and I will rule all space and time.' He laughed.

There was a crashing discord from the guitar, a thud from the drums, and silence.

Fitz was right in front of Ed now, but the huge man didn't

seem to have seen him.

'I've got a bomb!' yelled Fitz. His voice carried over the speaker system, generating a wail of feedback.

'So what?' said Ed. 'So has everybody else, at the moment. And it isn't going to save them, either.'

Behind him, Fitz heard a roaring noise. Faint, compared with the music, and he didn't recognise it at first. Then the mics picked it up, and the sound filled the stadium, straining through the amps.

The crowd were bewildered, but Fitz knew what it was. He watched as the TARDIS materialised in the middle of the stage, about twenty feet in front of Ed. The doors opened, and the Doctor emerged, followed by Maddie.

Maddie had Fitz's revolver planted firmly against the back of the Doctor's skull.

Chapter Twenty

The music was wonderful. Maddie wanted to dance, wanted to spin away into the huge space shown her by Om-Tsor. Ed was chanting:

'*I will be a Lord of Time and Space,*

'*I will rule the Destiny of the Human Race…*'

She could see his real body, standing above the lumpen flesh: shining, muscular, the guitar hanging around it. He'd given himself wings.

She saw him reach out, touch the complex space she'd made inside the TARDIS. His arms became endless, copies of arms running through the infinite mazes of the alien machinery.

The machine began to change, slowly at first, then more rapidly. Maddie could almost feel the power, the glory that would be Ed's.

Fitz glanced nervously about. The Doctor's face had a bleak look. A woman was running across the stage. She positioned herself behind Ed, caught hold of his chair – a wheelchair – and pushed him forward, past Fitz, towards the open door of the TARDIS. Around them, the stage was filling with people who had followed in Fitz and Sam's footsteps, clambering up from the crowd. People were shouting, confused. Fitz could hear the air-raid sirens, mixed with a long, deep rumble that he hoped was only thunder.

'No! Pippa!' Sam was struggling in the arms of the large man.

Fitz looked at the Doctor's face again, and knew that he had to do something. Now. He lifted the briefcase containing the bomb, watched the Doctor shake his head minimally.

Ed was almost at the TARDIS. Fitz realised he had no choice: he made a dive for Maddie and the gun.

The Doctor dropped at the same moment. Maddie didn't fire at once, instead tried to swing the gun to cover Fitz. He chopped at her wrist. It didn't work: the gun was still pointing at his chest.

Maddie didn't shoot.

Fitz hesitated, then clubbed her over the head with the briefcase. She dropped back, the gun went off, Fitz grabbed it. The barrel was hot in his hand. He twisted it round, took hold of the grip.

He looked up, to see Ed staring at him.

Without time to think, he aimed at the man's forehead and pulled the trigger.

'No!' shrieked Maddie. There were more screams from the crowd. People were running across the stage.

And a red flower was blooming in the middle of Ed Hill's forehead.

I've killed him, thought Fitz. His hands felt bruised where the gun had jumped in recoil.

Then, to Fitz's horror, Ed's eyes moved in their sockets, and he spoke. The voice boomed from everywhere, not just amplified electronically, but huge and real, as if he'd taken over the air itself. 'Now you've done it, baby.' An obscene giggle. 'A fatal wound. End of the world.'

Blood was flowing down Ed's face, dripping from his chin.

Behind him, the TARDIS began to get bigger.

'Oh, no,' shrieked the Doctor. 'No, no, no, no! The damage

you've done to his brain – he's completely out of control!'

A huge force caught Fitz and sent him flying backwards, rolling across the stage. He saw Sam fall: only the Doctor remained standing.

The Doctor bent down, picked up the gun.

Fitz saw it in flashes, as his body rolled away, helpless before the spreading force. The TARDIS was at least ten metres high, and it was distorting, melting like a huge blue candle. The Doctor was moving closer to Ed, the gun in his hand.

The gun against the back of Ed's neck.

There was a shot.

The Doctor's face twisted in agony, his jacket spattered with blood.

Then the Doctor was running, running towards Fitz. 'Into the TARDIS! Now! Now!'

Fitz scrambled up, ran towards the TARDIS, now slowly returning to normal. The door was still open. He almost fell over Ed's body, slumped in the chair. Blood was pooling around it. He walked through the door, and was surprised to see Maddie inside, standing by the console. Her face was white.

'He's dead, isn't he?'

Fitz nodded, realised he couldn't stop nodding.

'So there's no point.'

'No point?'

She shrugged, walked past Fitz, out of the TARDIS, without saying a word.

Belatedly, Fitz realised that the cloister bell was ringing.

Haystacks let Sam go at last, but only after it was obvious that Ed Hill was dead. Sam just stood there, staring at the sky, still not quite able to believe that she'd seen Fitz try to kill someone and the Doctor finish the job.

She could still see the Doctor's face at that moment, the horror written on it as he realised what he would have to do, what he *was doing*, what he *had done*.

Now the Doctor was yelling at Pippa: 'Om-Tsor! Where is it? Now!'

The woman hesitated, and the Doctor shouted, almost spitting, 'You've got thirty seconds before the first bomb goes off and five million people die! I also need to fix the TARDIS, unscramble the timelines, purge the Vortex if I can… Om-Tsor! *I need it now!*'

Haystacks ran across the stage, spoke briefly with the drummer. Sam noticed that the audience who'd clambered on to the stage were forming a rough circle around the set, watching.

The Doctor ran across to the drummer and picked up a small wooden chest. He simply gobbled down the contents without ceremony, then sat down, cross-legged, and closed his eyes.

There was a brief pause, and then the world seemed to tremble slightly, as if the air were water and a wave had moved across it. Clouds drifted over the stadium, and a thin rain began to fall. The Doctor still sat cross-legged. Sam went and stood by his side. She imagined him reaching into the space around the earth, tracking the missiles, the planes –

Would he kill the pilots of the planes?

No, she knew, somehow he would avoid it. He *would*. He could do miracles without killing.

But she looked down, and saw his jacket and face were still spattered with blood. She couldn't stop looking. Everything

244

else, everyone else, was silent. Waiting.

He opened his eyes, looked up at her, momentarily solemn. 'All done,' he said, and jumped up.

'Did you kill anyone else?'

The Doctor had already started towards the TARDIS. 'What?'

'You killed Ed.'

'He was dying!'

Sam just looked at him.

'I had no time!' he shouted. 'I had to save the TARDIS from Ed and the world from its own stupidity and…' He sounded mad, raving. 'There was no time to do anything else! No time!'

'You still killed him.' Sam was surprised at the edge of anger in her voice. She hadn't thought she could get angry this way, not with the Doctor.

'He did it!' A woman's voice, raw with anger and tears. Sam saw Maddie rushing across the stage towards them, flanked by two policemen. She was pointing at the Doctor. 'He killed Ed!'

Sam bundled the Doctor towards the TARDIS. 'There really wasn't time,' he was saying. 'Ed's interference was close to generating a critical instability in the Eye of Harmony. It could have been worse than the bombs – there might not have been any Earth left! Nothing, nothing, nothing…'

They were inside the TARDIS now. The Doctor ran to the console and slumped against one of the pillars, his eyes closed. Sam saw Fitz, gestured at the Doctor. She couldn't bring herself to speak to either of them.

Fitz ran up to the Doctor, grabbed his shoulders, shook them. 'Come on, Doctor!' he said. 'We've got to go!'

The Doctor looked up at him with hollow eyes, then

nodded and pulled a lever on the console. The time rotor began to move, just as Sam heard a distant banging on the outer doors.

The Doctor looked up at Sam, but she didn't smile.

Maddie watched as the Police Box thinned and vanished in the air in front of her, and clenched her fists in frustration.

'They've gone,' she said, unnecessarily, to the two bewildered policemen standing beside her. 'They killed him, and they've gone.'

One of the policemen coughed. 'Do you know who they were?'

Maddie ignored him. She knew what she had to do, and she had to do it now.

She went to Ed's body, and kneeled, dipped her finger in the sticky blood around his feet. With it, she drew a crude circle on her chest – it took several attempts – and a capital R inside the circle.

Then she went to the microphone, and began to speak to the assembled people.

'He died for you,' she said simply, 'And I want you to carry out his dream.'

She went on speaking then, telling them there would be no more war, that everyone should think only of peace and happiness, and that the flowers would grow everywhere, if only people tried hard enough to love one another.

As she spoke, the white light of the mountains seemed to fill her eyes.

Press Reports, 1969-73

The Daily Telegraph, 29 September 1969:

Several dozen young people were arrested today during a pop festival in East Worldham, Hampshire, arranged by the so-called 'Revolution Man' cult. Charges ranged from the possession of illegal drugs to gross indecency and assault.

The leader of the cult, Maddie Burton, was the friend of the murdered singer Ed Hill who claimed that he was the Revolution Man. She told me: 'The police have no place in a society where the rule of love is more important than the rule of law. Why do they think the event of last May happened? Does Ed Hill's death mean nothing to them?'

However local schoolmaster Nigel Leigh-Morgan commented that 'dancing naked in a field in broad daylight in front of respectable people is hardly likely to bring about a new age of peace and joy. These people should take their motorbikes and their drugs and their noise elsewhere.'

The Church Times, 14 August 1970:

Most of our readers will have heard of the so-called 'Revolution Man' cult. One of the more extraordinary cults to spring up following the dangerous international events of May last year, it is led by the charismatic Madeleine 'Maddie' Burton. A friend of the murdered singer Edward Hill, she claims that Hill was, in fact, the second coming of the Messiah, and intended to bring only peace and love to all mankind.

Whatever Miss Burton's claims, however, most dispassionate observers would note that it was largely the 'magical' activities of the Revolution Man in attacking the military installations of the United States and other powers that led to last May's conflict and to near disaster for all of us.

Her latest claim that Hill had a status akin to that of Our Lord Himself is not only blasphemous, it is dangerous, typical of the pernicious philosophies of the nineteen-sixties which are eating away at the heart of our society.

Le Monde, 12 December 1973:

The death was reported in Paris today of Madeleine 'Maddie' Burton, the English leader of the 'Revolution Man' cult. She had been ill for some time as a result of drug addiction.

The cult has been in decline for some time, with many of its members joining hippie communes and other communities peripheral to society. The death of Miss Burton will almost certainly mean the end of it.

Epilogue

'I don't agree,' said Sam.

Her face over the chessboard was stubborn. Neither she nor Fitz had moved a piece in nearly half an hour. Around them, Sam's room was tidy, a few clothes folded on the foot of the bed, a few small mementoes arranged neatly on shelves. She'd even tucked her boots under the foot of the bed.

'Look. Ed Hill was about to take over the TARDIS – or try to. You heard what the Doctor said. It could have destroyed the Earth.'

'That was because you shot him. You didn't have to do that. The Doctor needed the Om-Tsor, that was all. It could have been done without violence.' Sam's voice was flat, judgmental.

'The Doctor would never have got to it while Ed was still alive. Not in time. Anyway, Ed had tried to kill me once. He saw me with the gun. He was going to kill *me*.' He looked down at the chessboard desperately, remembered a move he'd considered, picked up a black rook.

Sam didn't even notice. She looked up, flushing with anger. 'And you made the Doctor finish the job.'

'He chose to.'

'He *never* chooses to kill. He didn't have any choice.'

'And neither did I.' said Fitz. 'Anyway, there wasn't time to think.'

He thought he'd won the point then, but Sam's cool eyes looked at his face, read his expression. 'It's not clever, Fitz,' she said quietly. 'It's taking life.'

'Ed was about to take millions of lives.'

'That's not the point. You're not sorry.'

'Of course I'm sorry!' Though he wasn't, actually. 'I just don't –' He broke off, unsure what he was saying. Sam was beginning to make him feel really angry. He stood up. 'I think I'll just take a walk, see if I can sort out –'

'You're not sorting anything out,' said Sam, 'You're running away from it. And *don't* bother the Doctor, he'll be feeling sick with guilt.'

'I've told you he chose to do it!' barked Fitz. 'You can't put all the blame on me!'

'He's a hero!' Sam was shouting too, now. 'And he never never never does anything wrong – you don't understand!'

'You're right!' snapped Fitz. 'I don't understand! I don't even want to be here!'

He turned on his heel and walked from the room, slamming the door behind him.

Fitz walked, and walked, and walked, through corridors that were high and arched with wood and glass, over a bridge that dropped to a chasm of crystal and silver, across a park full of tropical air and small, blue plants with spherical flowers like eyes. Eventually, he sat down on a bench in the park, and watched the plants watching him. There was a 'sky' above, ribbed with orange steel girders.

He searched in his coat pockets for a cigarette, failed to find any.

A universe, he thought. That's what's on offer here. That's what Ed Hill wanted – probably all he wanted in the first place, poor sod, before it all went wrong.

And I killed him, because I panicked. Sam's right.

He stood up, and slowly at first, then more quickly, he began to make his way back.

BBC DOCTOR WHO BOOKS

THE EIGHT DOCTORS *by Terrance Dicks* ISBN 0 563 40563 5
VAMPIRE SCIENCE *by Jonathan Blum and Kate Orman* ISBN 0 563 40566 X
THE BODYSNATCHERS *by Mark Morris* ISBN 0 563 40568 6
GENOCIDE *by Paul Leonard* ISBN 0 563 40572 4
WAR OF THE DALEKS *by John Peel* ISBN 0 563 40573 2
ALIEN BODIES *by Lawrence Miles* ISBN 0 563 40577 5
KURSAAL *by Peter Anghelides* ISBN 0 563 40578 3
OPTION LOCK *by Justin Richards* ISBN 0 563 40583 X
LONGEST DAY *by Michael Collier* ISBN 0 563 40581 3
LEGACY OF THE DALEKS *by John Peel* ISBN 0 563 40574 0
DREAMSTONE MOON *by Paul Leonard* ISBN 0 563 40585 6
SEEING I *by Jonathan Blum and Kate Orman* ISBN 0 563 40586 4
PLACEBO EFFECT *by Gary Russell* ISBN 0 563 40587 2
VANDERDEKEN'S CHILDREN *by Christopher Bulis* ISBN 0 563 40590 2
THE SCARLET EMPRESS *by Paul Magrs* ISBN 0 563 40595 3
THE JANUS CONJUNCTION *by Trevor Baxendale* ISBN 0 563 40599 6
BELTEMPEST *by Jim Mortimore* ISBN 0 563 40593 7
THE FACE EATER *by Simon Messingham* ISBN 0 563 55569 6
THE TAINT *by Michael Collier* ISBN 0 563 55568 8
DEMONTAGE *by Justin Richards* ISBN 0 563 55572 6

THE DEVIL GOBLINS FROM NEPTUNE *by Keith Topping and Martin Day*
ISBN 0 563 40564 3
THE MURDER GAME *by Steve Lyons* ISBN 0 563 40565 1
THE ULTIMATE TREASURE *by Christopher Bulis* ISBN 0 563 40571 6
BUSINESS UNUSUAL *by Gary Russell* ISBN 0 563 40575 9
ILLEGAL ALIEN *by Mike Tucker and Robert Perry* ISBN 0 563 40570 8
THE ROUNDHEADS *by Mark Gatiss* ISBN 0 563 40576 7
THE FACE OF THE ENEMY *by David A. McIntee* ISBN 0 563 40580 5
EYE OF HEAVEN *by Jim Mortimore* ISBN 0 563 40567 8
THE WITCH HUNTERS *by Steve Lyons* ISBN 0 563 40579 1
THE HOLLOW MEN *by Keith Topping and Martin Day* ISBN 0 563 40582 1
CATASTROPHEA *by Terrance Dicks* ISBN 0 563 40584 8
MISSION IMPRACTICAL *by David A. McIntee* ISBN 0 563 40592 9
ZETA MAJOR *by Simon Messingham* ISBN 0 563 40597 X
DREAMS OF EMPIRE *by Justin Richards* ISBN 0 563 40598 8
LAST MAN RUNNING *by Chris Boucher* ISBN 0 563 40594 5
MATRIX *by Robert Perry and Mike Tucker* ISBN 0 563 40596 1
THE INFINITY DOCTORS *by Lance Parkin* ISBN 0 563 40591 0
SALVATION *by Steve Lyons* ISBN 0 563 55566 1
THE WAGES OF SIN *by David A. McIntee* ISBN 0 563 55567 X
DEEP BLUE *by Mark Morris* ISBN 0 563 55571 8
PLAYERS *by Terrance Dicks* ISBN 0 563 55573 4

SHORT TRIPS *ed. Stephen Cole* ISBN 0 563 40560 0
MORE SHORT TRIPS *ed. Stephen Cole* ISBN 0 563 55565 3

THE NOVEL OF THE FILM *by Gary Russell* ISBN 0 563 38000 4

THE BOOK OF LISTS *by Justin Richards and Andrew Martin* ISBN 0 563 40569 4
A BOOK OF MONSTERS *by David J. Howe* ISBN 0 563 40562 7
THE TELEVISION COMPANION *by David J. Howe and Stephen James Walker*
ISBN 0 563 40588 0
FROM A TO Z *by Gary Gillatt* ISBN 0 563 40589 9